DOCTOR · WHO

Autonomy

DOCTOR·WHO

Autonomy

DANIEL BLYTHE

2 4 6 8 10 9 7 5 3 1

Published in 2009 by BBC Books, an imprint of Ebury Publishing
A Random House Group Company

© Daniel Blythe, 2009

Daniel Blythe has asserted his right to be identified as the author of this
Work in accordance with the Copyright, Design and Patents Act 1988.

Doctor Who is a BBC Wales production for BBC One
Executive Producers: Russell T Davies and Julie Gardner

Original series broadcast on BBC Television. Format © BBC 1963.
'Doctor Who', 'TARDIS' and the Doctor Who logo are trademarks of the
British Broadcasting Corporation and are used under licence.
Autons created by Robert Holmes.

The Random House Group Ltd Reg. No. 954009.
Addresses for companies within the Random House Group can be found
at www.randomhouse.co.uk.

A CIP catalogue record for this book is available from the British
Library.

ISBN 978 1 846 07759 3

The Random House Group Limited supports the Forest Stewardship
Council (FSC), the leading international forest certification organisation.
All our titles that are printed on Greenpeace approved FSC certified
paper carry the FSC logo. Our paper procurement policy can be found
at www.rbooks.co.uk/environment

Series Consultant: Justin Richards
Project Editor: Steve Tribe
Cover design by Lee Binding © BBC 2009

Typeset in Albertina and Deviant Strain
Printed and bound in Germany by GGP Media GmbH

To Ellie and Sam

'Hide your tie in your bag,' Kate said to Lisa, as they ascended the travelator with the other shoppers.

Lisa looked at her suspiciously. 'Why?'

Kate Maguire tutted and rolled her eyes. 'Because we're nicking off, you idiot! Hyperville's packed with CCTV. Anybody spots us, we'll be slung out!'

'Oh. Right.' Lisa Henshaw looked abashed, and pulled her St Mary's School tie off and shoved it into her bag.

Tall and graceful, in their smart white blouses and black skirts, the two teenage girls could just about have passed for shop-girls or young professionals. Kate's eyes flicked back and forth as she took in the crowds around them: a mixture of people, even now, midweek. Young and old, casual and formal, some mums with kids and some older people. All heading the same way. All heading for Hyperville – which was always alive, always packed, always echoing and light.

Kate's heart skipped a beat as she looked down through the glass tube of the travelator and saw the endless car parks, giving way in the distance to the fields and lakes. The world beyond Hyperville. And up ahead of them was the gaping, glittering maw of the place itself, smelling sweetly of some chemical aroma. And coffee.

'Come on,' she said to Lisa. 'Let's have some fun.'

Up on Seventh Boulevard, high in the top reaches of the ShopZone, Kate nodded to Lisa.

'They say they watch *everyone*. They say they can see everything everyone does in here.'

'Don't people mind?'

Kate shrugged. 'You know what things are like. It's 2009. All those things happening in London. Security alerts, aliens and stuff. People like it now. They like to feel safer.'

'You think?'

'Sure. Bet you, in four or five years' time they'll have armed police and we'll all be showing ID cards everywhere we go. Nobody minds – well, nobody except a few civil liberties cranks.'

They stood looking out at the bustling ShopZone. Lisa shook her head. 'Never realised how massive the place was.'

'Biggest in Europe,' said Kate with a grin. 'They're meant to be building others now, but this was the first. I used to come here as a little kid when it was being built. I used to sit on the hill with my binocs and watch the scaffolding going up for the Pyramid. You remember when it all started?'

'We were in primary school,' said Lisa absently, gazing out across the mall. 'And what the hell's *that*?' she added, pointing.

A metal sphere, like a mirrorball with a glowing blue underside, was bobbing above the shoppers. It swivelled like a jittery predator, its circumference bounded with a ring of red electronic eyes. It seemed to float on air, and to move with the swift, darting motion of a dragonfly.

'Japanese tech,' said Kate confidently. 'They call it an Oculator.'

'You're making that up.'

'Honest! I googled it. Found out all about it. It moves on tiny gas-jets. It looks like metal, but I think it's some sort of really light plastic.'

As if it could hear them, the Oculator whizzed over to their balcony, an electronic eye flipping up to stare straight at them. Lisa took an involuntary step backwards.

'I don't like it,' she said.

Kate laughed. 'Look normal,' she said. 'Smile at it. Like you're on *Big Brother*.'

And the Oculator's eye seemed to pulse, as if it had heard Kate's words.

Deep within the heart of Hyperville, silver walls curved to form a soft, enclosing chamber lined with monitor screens.

On his podium at the back of the room, like a captain on the bridge of his ship, Max Carson gripped the rail in front of him, surveying the technicians in their headsets. Thin-faced, with pale lips and slicked-back, coal-dark hair, he was a slim, bony man in his thirties, dressed in an expensive black suit and shirt with gold cufflinks. He wore a small, almost-invisible, clear plastic earpiece in each ear, like discreet iPod headphones.

Max Carson was newly appointed at Hyperville, in a role

broadly known as Director of Operations. Sir Gerry's aide, Miss Devonshire, had recommended Max highly. All Sir Gerry knew was that Hyperville had struggled before they had Max, and that now it seemed to run smoothly with oiled precision. Every organisation, Sir Gerry said, needed a Max.

'Seven, focus me that one.'

Max's voice was low, but a radio-mike in his collar carried it into the headphones of every operative.

One of the screens blossomed and grew, until it covered the entire chessboard of tiles – the face of a girl filling the room. She was smiling, arms folded as she looked into the camera.

Max stroked his chin thoughtfully. 'That young woman's here almost every week,' he said. 'I wonder about her. Seven, information.'

The operative's hands flickered over his keyboard and, an instant later, the young woman's picture was uploaded to the terminal in front of Max, together with a stream of data.

A voice chattered in Max's earpiece, and he nodded.

'Of course,' he said. 'Excellent idea.' He spoke into his collar-mike again. 'See if you can get her tagged. I'd like to track her.'

Kate and Lisa rode the escalator-tubes down to the corner of Ninth Boulevard and Western Avenue, to a plaza bathed in near-natural light, where a juggler and a fire-eater were entertaining awestruck small children and their parents.

Kate nodded to the softly lit waterfalls either side of the lift-tubes.

'See those?' she said. 'They're to make people feel calm. Shopping's stressful, but if they can get people to relax, they spend more.' She sniffed the air. 'And smell that.'

Lisa sniffed, nose in the air like a bloodhound. 'Coffee,' she said. 'And bread.'

Kate grinned. 'Yup. And a hint of jasmine. Just the right mix of smells, you see. Designed to get people calm and hungry. Perfect combination for making them shop.'

Lisa frowned. 'What, so they control all the smells of the different shops?'

'Don't be daft.' Kate pointed to the grilles set into the floor at even intervals. 'They pump it out of there.' She nodded upwards. 'More right up in the dome, too, I bet. All computerised. They're moving towards having the whole thing switched to one central system in a few years. Imagine that. This whole artificial city run by one microchip.' She shook her head in awe. 'It's just brilliant.'

'How do you know so much about this place?' Lisa asked.

'Remember our free project work for Cultural?' said Kate. 'Most people chose boring film stars and bands and stuff. Me, I did Hyperville.'

'You're kidding.'

'Nope.'

'You *loser*.'

Kate wasn't bothered by Lisa's insults. 'Nah, it's fascinating. I want to be an investigative journalist, Lisa. I want it to be my job to find this kind of thing out.'

'Really?'

'Yes.' Kate shivered a little with excitement. 'And this is the future, Lisa, babe. Whether we like it or not.'

Lisa folded her arms. 'I don't really like it. I prefer the open air. Give me a nice park any day.'

Kate thought of the parks near where she and her mum lived – covered in graffiti, full of dog mess, and with hoodies laughing and smoking and kicking cans around the playground. She couldn't see how anybody could prefer that to somewhere like this.

'Scuse me?'

Kate and Lisa turned round at the voice behind them. Kate sized up the owner of the voice – a tall, lanky, youngish bloke with tousled brown hair, who was peering at a brochure through squarish spectacles. There was something mischievous about his face, she thought, as if he knew more than he was letting on. She wondered whether to tell him that Converse trainers with a brown pinstripe suit was a bit Nineties, but she decided against it.

'Yes?' she said.

'Trying to find my way into the FunGlobe,' he said. 'Every time I come here, I keep meaning to look at it. FunGlobe. *Fun-Gloooobe.*' He seemed to roll the word around his mouth. 'I mean, I can't really resist a name like that.'

'It's all on the map,' said Kate, and she took the map from the stranger's hands and replaced it – the right way up. 'Just a question of reading it right.'

Behind his glasses, the young man's eyes lit up. 'Oh, I see!' He slapped his forehead theatrically. 'I'm so thick sometimes.' He grinned – a big, genuine, white grin, showing fine teeth. 'Oh! By the way…' He fished in his suit pocket and drew something out, offering it to Kate.

She recoiled instantly. 'Why are you giving me that?'

'Um, well. There's a good reason. Trust me. Sort of… future investment. You'd never believe me if I actually told you. Honestly.'

She looked at it. Glossy, slim, curved at the edges, the credit card looked like a futuristic version of the Hypercard, the easy plastic currency which everyone loaded up with pounds and used in the complex.

She found herself meekly taking it. There was something about this man which invited trust.

'Thank you!' he said.

'You're welcome,' muttered Kate.

'Look after it.'

The man swivelled on his heel and disappeared into the crowd.

Lisa shook her head. 'You see, that's the other thing about this kind of place. Weirdos.'

Kate was staring thoughtfully in the direction the man had gone.

'I don't think he was a weirdo,' she said. 'It was like he was trying to *tell* me something.'

She stared down at the Hypercard and, almost without thinking, tucked it away in an inside pocket.

'Coffee?'

A Chinese woman had appeared at Kate's elbow, smiling and offering cardboard cups of coffee on a tray. 'New promotion, courtesy of Hyperville? Free samples?'

'I could do with a coffee,' Kate said, and took one. 'Thanks.'

Lisa, arms folded, shook her head.

The Chinese woman smiled, bobbed and turned away. 'Have a good day,' she said, as Kate took a sip.

The coffee was full, rich and warming, with a hint of spiciness – it tasted *real*, Kate thought, not synthetic like some of the stuff she had at home and not too milky like the ones in the local cafés.

'Mmm,' she said. 'Good stuff.'

The coffee seemed to power into her body, warming her from within.

She felt good. But then Kate Maguire always felt good when she came to Hyperville.

ONE

'**A**ttention. Attention. This is Hyperville. Good morning to all customers. We would like to draw your attention to today's special offer. Holders of red 300-euro Hypercards are entitled to a free half-day session in the Spa and Pool Complex until 12 noon on Thursday. Unwind, float and enjoy a world of water at Hyperville. Shop. Dream. Relax.'

Behind a huge, polished desk, Sir Gerry Hobbes-Mayhew surveyed his empire.

From his office in the apex of Hyperville's central pyramid, he could look out on the complex from the picture window: the metallic triangle of the ShopZone, the glass dome of the FunGlobe, the comings and goings of the many travelators and shuttle buses. Hyperville was miles from the nearest city – that was deliberate. People sometimes booked themselves in for three, four, five days at a time – you couldn't have them disappearing off and not spending money. Everything they wanted was here.

His intercom buzzed.

'Ey up?' he said, half-closing his crumpled eyes.

The plasma screen, taking up all of the far wall of his office, showed the dark, goatee-bearded face of Max Carson. 'Sir Gerry, that journalist is here again. Andrea Watkins.'

Sir Gerry sighed, puffed his florid red cheeks. That wretched girl. She'd done an interview with him for *Metropolitan* a few months ago – a puff piece, very nice, all about his taste in art and his philanthropic tendencies – but ever since then she had been plaguing him for a follow-up. She wouldn't leave him alone.

'What the 'eck's she after now, Max?'

'She's asking about the accident.'

Sir Gerry spread his hands. 'They've had the official inquiry,' he growled. 'What does she want, Max? Blood?'

Max smiled. 'She says she's going to the authorities if she doesn't have her questions answered, Sir Gerry.'

'The *authorities*. Cheek of t'lass. Does she even know who the "authorities" are? When the country's plagued with bomb threats and supposed alien invasions…'

'Well, quite, sir.'

'She thinks they're going to be bothered about one poor daft feller who got himself electrocuted through some dodgy wiring?'

'She seems very insistent, Sir Gerry.'

'Rule One, Max. Insistent people need to be dealt with. So deal with her.' Sir Gerry lit one of his huge cigars and leaned back in his chair, wreathed in clouds of blue smoke.

Max smiled again. 'Very good, Sir Gerry.'

'And Max,' Sir Gerry added, puffing on the cigar, 'how long until them wretched apprentices get 'ere?'

'The Trainees will arrive in one hour and fifty-eight minutes, Sir Gerry.'

Sir Gerry grunted his approval. In the four years since he'd been brought in, Max had proved his efficiency, but sometimes he could be just a little too pedantic. Most people would have said two hours, and been happy with that.

'Champion. Be sure you send 'em straight to me when they arrive.'

The screen went dark.

Sir Gerry sighed, hauled himself up from his seat and waddled over to the cylindrical drinks cabinet in the centre of the room. 'Single malt,' he growled. 'No ice.' The machine clunked and whirred, and a second later it had dispensed a crystal glass with a double shot of Sir Gerry's favourite spirit.

'Don't like interfering types,' Sir Gerry muttered to himself into his whisky. 'Don't like 'em at all.'

Arranged in a perfect equilateral triangle, with the hub of a big, well-known store at each of the points, Hyperville's ShopZone was a vast, glittering consumer palace, packed with strolling people. Pellucid blue escalator-tubes criss-crossed the ceiling above, their passengers like sea-life in an aquarium. Avalanches of vermilion foliage spilled from latticed balconies. High above the malls was a dome, its neo-classical *trompe l'œil* skyscape a bright shade of sapphire. A soft babble of voices carried upwards, occasionally punctuated by the bing-bong of the public address system.

Off the bustling, soft-white space of Europa Plaza was the Holistic HealthZone, with its endless arcades of organic fruit shops, ethical cosmetics and natural remedies. And in an alcove by a service door stood a rickety blue police box. It was looking as inconspicuous as it was possible for something so anachronistic to look.

The box's sole occupant popped his tousled head out of the door, eyes wide, and sniffed the air. 'Coffee, bread, hint of jasmine,' he murmured to himself. 'Okaaaay. Definitely the right place.'

The Doctor stepped out of the TARDIS and swivelled on one heel, taking a quick look at the bustling, brightly lit square beyond.

Most people would not have looked twice at his chosen outfit of pinstripe suit, dark shirt and loose tie, although the trainers which accompanied it might have given them pause for thought. If anyone asked, the Doctor would explain that this was because he often had to do a lot of running. If they ever asked why, they soon found out.

'Here we go, then.' The Doctor turned round, snapped his fingers and the TARDIS door squeaked, then slammed shut. He grinned, as much in surprise as in satisfaction. 'Getting better at that,' he said.

A quick glance at some calendars in a nearby gift shop was enough to tell him that the year was 2013. He liked to trust the TARDIS to get him to the right place and time these days, but it had been known to overshoot by a hundred years, or even a hundred million years. Which could be both embarrassing and inconvenient.

Hands in pockets, grinning, brown eyes wide open in admiration, the Doctor sauntered through Hyperville.

He'd seen leisure and shopping palaces before, of course. He remembered a particularly impressive one on stilts above the swamps of Dargeb IV, and an underwater retail experience beneath the carmine oceans of Ororous's second moon. But there was something very special, he always thought, about the ideas Earth people came up with. Something energetic, interesting, almost quaint. And the people themselves were usually a delight, even if the officious ones in uniform did cause him a bit of bother. The Doctor didn't always admit as much, but he did quite like humans. They were sometimes his favourite species.

This place seemed incredible for the time. The Doctor had checked the computerised maps and had realised that Hyperville covered an area of something like five square miles. The basic layout was a huge, metal triangle, from the outside a glittering wall of silver. It had a cylindrical, ten-storey megastore at each apex, the shops between them selling practically every commodity known to the human race. Within the walkways, malls and plazas in the sides of the triangle lurked designer clothes boutiques, shops and coffee-lounges, along with the banks, chemists, delicatessens and other outlets expected by the visitor.

In each of the major Plazas – Europa, Australis and Afrika – there was a giant installation. Europa had a glittering, ice-smooth cliff of glass, fifty metres high and inlaid with continuously falling cobalt-blue water, like a great slab of sea looking out over the small figures of the shoppers. Australis had sixteen pillars of blood-red marble, curving upwards to meet at a single point above the square. And Afrika Plaza had a great globe the size of a house, made out of some translucent material, suspended on a filigree of near-invisible threads so that it appeared to float in mid-air.

At the centre of the triangle squatted the Pyramid, home

to the administration centre of Hyperville. And then beyond the apex of the triangle was the golden FunGlobe, which contained, as far as the Doctor could tell, a huge theme park: every themed leisure and fun permutation humans could think of.

The Doctor wasn't sure what he thought, to be honest. Part of him felt it showed great imagination and verve, but another part of him was disturbed by it. He wondered why the human race needed this artifice when they had, despite all their best efforts to contaminate it, a beautiful planet full of mountains and oceans and forests and beaches, many of them still unexplored. And that which disturbed him intrigued him. There was a story here. Something going on under the surface.

'Watch where you're going, mister!'

The Doctor stepped back, and looked down. Among the crowds streaming past him, he had almost failed to see the chubby teenage boy with cropped hair who was looking up at him belligerently, waving an ice cream in his face.

The Doctor smiled. 'Sorry. In my own world.'

'Yeah, well. You almost made me drop my ice cream. I could have sued you under Regulation 4.4 of the Personal Space Act.'

The Doctor looked puzzled. 'Personal Space… No, never mind.'

'Reece! Reece!' A screeching voice cut across the Doctor's thoughts, and he saw a girl with pulled-back blonde hair and saucer-sized earrings, wearing a pastel-pink psychedelic dress. She was heading towards them from one of the nearby escalator-tubes, beckoning angrily at the boy. 'We're gonna be late for the Doomcastle! Come on!'

The Doctor looked at the boy sympathetically. 'Sister?'

The boy nodded sheepishly. 'Chantelle. Gotta go.'

'Er…what is the… Doomcastle, exactly?'

The boy Reece held his ice cream mid-lick, managing to point it at the Doctor in a way which suggested he was beneath contempt. 'You don't know?' he said. 'What channels do you watch?'

'Oh, I haven't seen any decent telly in ages. Last thing I saw was that girl playing noughts-and-crosses, you know, with the…' The Doctor paused, finger in mid-air describing a noughts-and-crosses grid. 'With the clown… You…have *no* idea what I'm talking about, do you?'

The boy shrugged, licking his ice cream.

The Doctor sighed. 'Never mind, I get used to that. So, look, come on, what *is* the Doomcastle?'

Chantelle folded her arms and narrowed her eyes at the Doctor. 'Why don't you buy a ticket, mate?' she sneered. 'You might find out. Only fifty euros.' And she nodded to the electronic ticket booth at the side of the escalator. 'You need to get a move on, though. Train leaves in ten minutes.'

The Doctor pulled a face, bobbed his head from side to side as if weighing the idea up. 'Ten minutes. Right. OK.' He put his glasses on and leaned down to peer at the electronic ticket booth, which resembled a tall, silver pyramid. It had a globe-shaped control panel on the top and a letterbox-sized slot. The screen on the panel was displaying a message in green pixels: INSERT CASH OR HYPERCARD. The Doctor tutted. 'This thing needs money.' He patted his pockets. 'Why do I *never* have money?'

He flipped his sonic screwdriver elegantly from his top pocket, jammed it up against the control panel and gave the dispenser a short, intense burst, looking guiltily over his shoulder. A young couple behind him did not seem to be paying him any attention at all. The machine clunked, whirred, and hiccupped. He selected his option on the screen, pressed the green button and took his ticket from the letterbox-slot as it was printed out. As he pocketed the ticket, the machine gave another hiccup and every light on the globe-shaped control panel was extinguished.

The young couple behind the Doctor, waiting patiently for their turn, looked disappointed. 'Is it not working?' asked the young man.

The Doctor rubbed his ear. 'Um, well, noooo. Think they've got a few, um, distribution problems in the system. You know. Credit crunch.'

He hopped into the blue tube and stood on the moving pavement, letting himself be carried through Hyperville towards Australis Plaza and an appointment with the Doomcastle.

High above him, a silvery globe, which appeared to be bouncing on air, sparkled and bleeped as it recorded every last pixel of the Doctor's face and flipped it through the network.

'Play it again, thirty-four,' said Max Carson sternly.

High on his platform overlooking the CCTV operatives, Max Carson sat in the black leather swivel-chair from which he usually worked. He wore a dark suit – a designer one these days, not the off-the-peg number he had owned four years ago when he first came to Hyperville – and he still had the same burning dark eyes and jet-black hair and beard, a little greyer now at the edges.

The walls flickered and danced with the images of a

thousand plasma screens, which covered the walls in ranks like electronic tiles. Two dozen young men and women wearing headsets sat at curved consoles, constantly monitoring the screen's output from computer terminals.

In the four years since Max had first arrived at Hyperville, this section had expanded into a full circle of screens and operatives. Every wall around him was relaying crisp images of the various sectors of Hyperville: the shopping, entertainment, leisure, sport and recreation zones. At night, the images would change, with fewer images from the shopping and sport zones and more from the casinos and nightclubs buried in Hyperville's lower levels.

The young operative addressed by Max obeyed his instruction. She flicked a switch and the footage appeared on his personal screen.

'What an unusual man,' he murmured, leaning forward.

The camera shot came from inside one of the electronic ticket booths, and showed a youngish man with tousled hair, black-rimmed glasses and an irreverent grin. He was leaning into the camera – so into the machine – and appeared to be poking about at it with some sort of screwdriver-like device which lit up at the end.

'What did he do, thirty-four?' Max asked calmly.

The answer crackled in Max's ear. 'He forced a focused sonic wave into the sub-utility governing Ticket Booth 297, sir. Introduced a malleability routine into the program that enabled him to obtain a ticket without Hypercard payment.'

Max Carson's face lit up in an unexpected smile. 'A proper criminal! Excellent. It's been a while since we've had one of those. It's been all common thugs and hoodlums these past few weeks.' He pressed his fingers together. 'I wonder what he's up to? A sonic device…Got to admit, that does show a certain touch of class.'

'Shall I get Captain Tilbrook to pull him in, sir?'

'No, no. Just watch him. I'm intrigued. I want to see what he does. Get his face cross-matched with the criminal ID databases. And see if you can find out what that device he used might actually be.'

'Very good, sir. And shall I inform Sir Gerry?'

Max frowned. 'Goodness, no. We don't need to worry the old fool. He's got enough on his plate with the Trainees arriving, not to mention that ridiculous pop-star woman.' He rose from his chair. 'Keep me informed of developments. I've got… another matter to attend to.'

Max flicked a switch on the arm of his chair – and his platform, complete with chair, descended slowly into the floor. After a few seconds, he had disappeared from view.

Andrea Watkins didn't like being kept waiting.

She was pacing up and down in the lobby, tapping her electronic notepad impatiently against her ring finger.

Her shiny high boots and tight leather-look skirt – both expensive items from a designer boutique called Zarasti – reflected the soft lighting. Occasionally she would glance through the impressive viewing window at the streaming hordes below in the mall. People in pastel hues and casuals, or crisp work suits, all going in and out of shops and carrying glossy, bulging bags emblazoned with the Hyperville logo and the name of the relevant shop. She could hear the hubbub, like a constant murmur in the background.

Andrea smiled. She enjoyed shopping.

The place was such a huge success, and that was supposed

to impress her – but it worried her. And it worried her editor, too. And so, as she already had an 'in' with Sir Gerry, she had been dispatched back to Hyperville to get the full story.

At the age of 41, unmarried and dedicated to her work, Andrea was desperate to find the story that would really put her name on the map. She was convinced that she was right on the brink of getting it.

The lift doors opened, and a dapper, bearded man emerged.

'Hello, Miss Watkins.'

Andrea remembered Max Carson, Sir Gerry's right-hand-man – she hadn't liked him when she first met him and she didn't like him now.

Behind him came a woman – elegant, her brown hair in a bun and her curvaceous form contained within a smart suit with matching heels. She wore an expensive gold watch and diamond earrings. Catlike green eyes surveyed Andrea from behind semi-rimless glasses. The woman said nothing.

Andrea decided in a second that she neither liked nor trusted the woman. Max Carson was just a smarmy businessman with a high opinion of himself – Andrea knew the type and could deal with them. But this woman was something different…something not quite *right*.

'Mr Carson,' said Andrea. She nodded to Max, and looked the woman up and down.

'Call me Max, please.' He gripped her hand warmly. He gestured to the smart woman. 'Oh, my associate, Miss Elizabeth Devonshire. She'll sit in on this meeting, if that's all right with you.'

Miss Devonshire was too sharp-looking, Andrea thought – too unnaturally immaculate. Andrea managed a tight, formal smile. 'Is Sir Gerry not available today?' she asked.

'Ah, well, the Chief Exec has a lot on his plate right now.' Max Carson beamed.

Miss Devonshire spoke. She had a warm, down-to-earth American accent. 'This is a big place, Andrea. Needs leadership and that, ah, special factor.'

'I hear he's auditioning for successors,' Andrea suggested impishly.

Max smiled. 'Not as such. Sir Gerry is instigating a rolling programme of intensive Management Training. He believes our young people are the future. As, indeed, do we.' Max gestured towards the office door. 'Perhaps you'd care to step inside?'

Andrea smiled. She didn't like this pair, but she would pretend to if it got her the story. 'Of course,' she said primly. Boots clicking on the wooden floor, she strode through the doorway.

Inside the office was a huge, oval table, an empty slab of polished wood. Andrea could not resist running her hands over it. Then she looked up. There were two muscled, black-uniformed security men standing either side of Max Carson's chair, their faces strangely impassive under their black baseball caps.

'Do they need to be here?' she asked.

Max Carson merely smiled and gestured expansively as he sat down. It was Miss Devonshire who answered the question.

'Standard procedure in these frightening times, Andrea. I do apologise. We wish as much as you do that we could live without such… measures.'

Andrea pulled a document from her handbag and spread

it out on the table in front of her. 'I have the originals of these documents in a safe place,' she said. Her heart was beating furiously at this moment of brazen confrontation, wondering how they would react. 'Documentation from the independent electrical contractors who checked your systems following the workman's death. As you can see, they indicate that there was no fault.' She pressed her fingers together. 'Just how did he die? Was it something to do with the new development of Plastinol-2?'

Max Carson raised an eyebrow. 'Plastinol-2?' He glanced at Miss Devonshire, who didn't react. 'Goodness. You have been doing your homework. Most journalists these days seem to think half an hour on Wikipedia will do.' He reached out a hand. 'May I?' he asked.

Andrea pushed the documents across the table to him. He scanned them, his eyes seeming to move very fast. She watched him. She was sure she had him rattled now, underneath that smooth surface. He then passed the documents to Miss Devonshire, who read them with a superior smile.

Andrea knew a lot didn't add up about the electrician who had died in the WinterZone. And she knew it had to be more than just coincidence that the cover-up had come now – just when Hyperville's investment in a new, pliable, versatile artificial substance called Plastinol-2 had come along. An investment which had a lot to do with Max Carson – and his former company, Carson Polymers. She wasn't sure where this creepy Devonshire woman fitted in, either.

After a minute or so, Miss Devonshire nodded and placed the papers back on the table in front of them.

'Seems you may be right,' she said softly. 'What are you gonna do with this information, Andrea?'

Andrea smiled. 'What any good journalist does. Check more sources, compile a devastating article, and publish.'

Max Carson's eyes, beneath his thick eyebrows, fixed on Andrea. Unnerved, Andrea glanced up at the two security men, still standing at ease either side of Max, hands clasped behind their backs. Their faces were glistening as if with sweat, but looked oddly waxy and rigid.

'I see,' said Max Carson eventually. 'You do realise, Miss Watkins, that any attempt to take on the power of Hyperville will almost certainly result in disaster?'

Andrea wrinkled her nose. 'That sounds like a threat.'

Max Carson beamed and spread his hands. 'Merely a friendly warning. Really. Forget this silly incident. Forget Plastinol-2. It's... at a very *early* research stage, shall we say. And go back to profiling your emerging businesswomen and your garden-shed businesses. They really are fascinating.'

'Max is being polite,' said Miss Devonshire. 'I think they're dull as heck, myself.'

Andrea was on her feet. She'd heard enough. She knew now that she wanted to take down this arrogant pair, and that she was going to enjoy doing it. 'You're very patronising, Mr Carson. And you, Miss Devonshire, you're just *rude*.' She turned her back to them and looked over her shoulder. 'I'll see myself out,' she said, and thumped the control to release the sliding doors.

It didn't work. Andrea thumped it again. No response. She sighed and turned back towards Max Carson. 'Mr Carson,' she said, 'this is very tire—'

She frowned. Max Carson was on his feet now, arms folded, and the two security men had lifted their right arms so that they were pointing at her in an accusing manner.

'What is this?' Andrea demanded. For the first time, now, her anger was giving way to fear.

'Accidents happen, Andrea,' said Miss Devonshire's drawl. It seemed to come from somewhere else, as if it was not really Miss Devonshire speaking to her, but someone – something – using her mouth and vocal cords. 'Even to visitors.'

Andrea, shaking, flipped out her mobile phone.

'Er, that won't work in here, I'm afraid,' said Max. 'Andrea. A moment, please. Put the phone away.' He gestured, then looked at Miss Devonshire as if expecting her to take the lead. He was sweating.

Andrea slowly folded her phone again and slipped it back into her bag.

Miss Devonshire came forward and leaned on the desk.

'You know what we do here,' said Miss Devonshire. 'You've researched our services. Dammit, you even know about Plastinol-2. That makes you interesting, Andrea. That makes you dangerous. Someone who can't be allowed to run around bleating about "accidents", unfortunately.' She glanced down at her boots and skirt. 'Hey, you shop at Hyperville. You're wearing one of our in-house brands. Zarasti, isn't it?'

Andrea slouched, hand on hip. 'What of it?'

'Zarasti fashions, as I'm sure you know, have the look and feel of the most expensive patent leather. But in fact, they're based on an early form of the Plastinol-2 compound.'

Andrea folded her arms crossly. 'I'm vegan. I don't wear leather. Your point?'

Miss Devonshire smiled and straightened up.

Max snapped his fingers, and the waxy-faced security men both lowered their arms in unison.

Miss Devonshire turned the dial of her gold watch.

At first, nothing seemed to happen.

And then, Andrea Watkins realised that she could not move her feet. The Plastinol boots around her feet had tightened, squashing her toes, pinning her to the spot.

Max and Miss Devonshire stood side by side and exchanged a satisfied look.

'The molecular structure of Plastinol is very pliable,' murmured Max Carson. 'An extremely versatile compound.'

Andrea's boots had lost their soft, leather-like comfort, and had become chilly and clammy. She was standing in cold, plasticky mud. She stared down in horror at her legs. The boots were *alive*. They were growing, climbing over her knees and moulding themselves to the outline of her legs. A squelching, slurping sound filled the room as the boots pinned her to the spot and began to engulf her.

'Stop this!' Andrea snapped, now more in outrage than in fear. She glowered angrily at Max and Miss Devonshire. 'Stop it immediately!'

'All right,' said Max Carson with a smile. He turned to Miss Devonshire. 'I think Miss Watkins knows we mean business, Elizabeth.'

But Miss Devonshire did not seem to hear him.

Max cleared his throat and glanced nervously at his associate. 'Elizabeth! I, ah, think that's enough!'

'It's not enough,' said Miss Devonshire. 'Zarasti fashion is rather wonderful. In fact, one might almost say it's *to die for*.'

The skirt tightened around Andrea's waist, making her gasp for breath. It had acquired the same pitchy, clammy feel as the boots, and was spreading outwards in both directions like a living thing. It was shimmering, swelling, slurping, as if alive and hungry.

Andrea felt her chest and stomach tightening. Her heart thumped in panic. '*Stop this now*!' she yelled.

Max licked his lips nervously, and looked from Andrea to Miss Devonshire and the guards and back again. 'Elizabeth,' he said. 'Look, come *on*. We agreed. We were just going to give her a little scare.'

'And so we are,' said Miss Devonshire, smiling.

The skirt-shape met up with the boot-shapes, forming one great mass of shiny Plastinol over the lower half of Andrea's body – and within seconds she found herself totally unable to move.

The Plastinol grew, expanded like spilled ink across her. She struggled, but it was like fighting something which was part of her skin.

'You can't do this!' Andrea screamed. 'You can't do this! What are you doing? *Stop it*!'

She watched as the Plastinol spread down her arms and encased her fingers, like the sleekest of evening-gloves. It tightened on her body, painful and grasping. She felt the coldness spreading to her neck. Now her entire body, up as far as the chin, was engulfed in glossy black plastic, spreading like a fluid to every extremity of her body.

With her eyes open wide in terror, the last thing Andrea Watkins saw was the burning, intense stare of Miss Devonshire, flanked by the impassive security men.

And then the slurping, clammy Plastinol engulfed her face, and she screamed.

Until it covered her mouth.

Then she stopped.

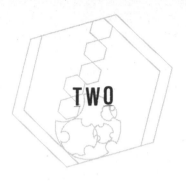

TWO

'Hello again!' said the Doctor to Reece and Chantelle Stanford, as he made his way down the aisle of the rickety wooden train. It didn't just run to the Doomcastle, he had noticed – rails ran all through the various zones of Hyperville, and you could book a tour through the whole lot if you were so inclined. The Doctor sat himself behind the teenagers, sprawling out with his feet up. 'Well, this is all right, isn't it? Nice comfy seats. I like a comfy seat.'

Chantelle shot a nervous smile at him.

Across the aisle, a rotund blonde woman and a grey-haired man turned and peered at the Doctor over matching red-framed glasses.

'Me mum,' Chantelle said. 'And Derek. He's her boyfriend.'

'Hello!' The Doctor waved, giving them an open-mouthed grin. They smiled nervously back. 'Ohhhh, I love stuff like this.

This is great, isn't it?' The Doctor looked round the carriage, but the other passengers – families with children, mainly – were ignoring him.

The locomotive didn't appear to have a real driver – just an animatronic mannequin, dressed in a shiny blue plastic suit and peaked cap. It had turned its head to greet all the passengers as they entered. The train sat on sturdy rails beside a platform, and through the open windows the Doctor could see the gaping mouth of the Doomcastle gate, into which the rails disappeared.

'*Ladies and gentlemen,*' said a voice through the speaker-grille at the front of the carriage. '*Your tour around the Doomcastle is about to begin. Please hold tight.*'

'Don't be sick this time, Reece,' said Chantelle to her brother. She looked round at the Doctor, grinning. 'He was sick at Alton Towers,' she said in hushed tones. 'Never saw nothing like it. Managed to hit some of the people six carriages behind.'

'Chantelle!' Reece thumped his sister's elbow. 'Shut *up!*'

'He shouldn't have had that ice cream,' muttered Chantelle, shaking her head. 'This is scarier than Alton Towers.'

The Doctor leaned forward. 'Have you been on this before?' he asked.

'Oh, yeah. Me and my mates come here all the time.'

The Doctor heard Mrs Stanford tutting and saw her shake her head.

Derek gave the Doctor a look which clearly said *Kids, eh?*

The Doctor made a token 'aaah-huh' sound and smiled. He didn't want to get into that debate right now. He leaned back towards Chantelle. 'How do you, um, pay, exactly?' he asked, intrigued.

Chantelle fished in her bag and showed him a small red card, the size and shape of a credit card. 'Hypercard,' she said. 'You pay for everything here on it. Saves carrying cash. Charge it up with euros and away you go. You can even plug it into your phone – look.' She showed the Doctor the bottom of her cellphone, which had a thin Hypercard-sized slot in it – she pushed the card in and pulled it out again.

'Could I have a look?'

'No.' Chantelle snapped her bag shut again. 'What's it to you, anyway?'

The Doctor pulled a face. 'Just interested.'

At that second, the train hooted and steam began to gather in clouds around them. The Doctor sprawled back in his seat, hands behind his head, and grinned.

'*Allons-y!*' he said delightedly.

Chantelle gave him a withering look.

The carriage juddered, the engine roared, and they were all slammed back into their seats as the train lurched into the darkness.

'*Attention. Attention. This is Hyperville. All ticket-holders for the Shaneeqi book-signing should make their way to Europa Plaza before 3pm. A blue Hypercard entitles you to twenty per cent off the price of Shaneeqi's new book… If you are shopping on Obama Boulevard today, then check out the styles in the Zarasti spring range – designer names at prices you can afford. Shop. Dream. Relax.*'

A glass lift powered its way up from the ShopZone, containing a sweating Sir Gerry and four smartly suited, fresh-looking young people.

The younger of the women was Kate Maguire. Encased in

pinstripes, elegantly made-up, with designer glasses, Kate felt older than her twenty years, but she was starting to wonder what she had let herself in for. Her heart was pounding.

The two young men, Alex and James, looked as if they'd come out of some business cloning factory, she decided, all hair-gel and neat ties and Armani suits, while her fellow female Trainee, Rhiannon, cut a striking figure in a cream jacket and skirt.

'Have a good look,' said Sir Gerry affably, wiping his brow with a spotted handkerchief, and gesturing below them at the ant-like hordes on the floor of the Mall. 'Rule One – always get a decent perspective on your business.'

Kate swallowed hard and pressed herself up against the lift wall. The glass-floored elevator seemed like a clever idea, but it played tricks with your mind, making you think you were about to fall.

At last, they arrived. The lift door hissed open and they stepped out, one by one, into the pale blue corridor. They were ushered past Sir Gerry's secretary and into his office, where they all stood, rigid like mannequins.

Sir Gerry cleared his throat and took a seat at his desk, flanked by a prim-looking aide. Kate thought the woman looked like her old school headmistress – fortyish, hair in a tight bun, smart suit, semi-rimless glasses.

'Welcome to Hyperville,' Sir Gerry began. 'Now, then. A few things which you should bloomin' well already know…'

Kate was still nervous, but made herself listen as the Chief Exec reeled off the history of Hyperville and all its achievements.

It was four years since she had shoved her tie in her bag, skipping school to come and see the place in all its glory. If only Sir Gerry knew, she thought, with a little smile, that she was the girl who, even earlier, had done her school project on the place – and who, still further back in time, had sat on the hills overlooking the site and watched it being constructed.

Kate couldn't remember a time when Hyperville hadn't been part of her life. She looked around at the other three, wondering if they were all thrusting young executives or business-school hotshots – or if they, like her, were in dead-end jobs and seizing with both hands the chance to do something better.

And she wondered if anyone would guess why she was really there.

'I'm going to get you all to do some teamwork and some tasks as the days go on,' said Sir Gerry. 'But first off, I want to know how good you are at sizing this place up. At giving *me* some advice. So – I want each of you to explore Hyperville. Do a report, with figures, to be on me desk in forty-eight hours' time. Tell me what's doing well, what's doing not-so-well, and where I could be earning *more money*. Use your eyes, your ears and your common sense. If you've got any. Equipment, please, Miss Devonshire.'

He nodded to the bespectacled aide, who pushed three perspex boxes across the desks. One contained four ID badges, the second four glossy black credit cards, and the third had four computer memory sticks inside.

'Access All Areas badges for you all,' said Miss Devonshire in a soft American drawl. 'And your Hypercards, which double as your room keys. And finally, some extensive notes and rules compiled by Sir Gerry for you all.'

'And damn well *read* 'em!' snapped Sir Gerry. 'They're not just for decoration. You can spend money to do your research

– but careful. They've got a limit. I'm not going to tell you what it is – up to you to find that out!' He tapped his head, chuckling. 'Bit of the old grey matter again. Any questions?'

Everyone was oddly silent. Kate bit her lip as she clipped her Access All Areas badge to her lapel. She wondered if she ought to ask something, or if that would be a sign of not having done her research properly. Or worse.

She became aware that Miss Devonshire was staring at her. She didn't think Miss Devonshire had blinked *at all* in the past few minutes. Kate's heart rate increased and her palms began to sweat. There was something else about Miss Devonshire's eyes. They were not just looking intently at her – they were glaring, fiercely alive. The blackness within them was fiery, as if burning with the power of some alien intelligence.

Kate broke her gaze away from Miss Devonshire, and cleared her throat.

'Yes?' Sir Gerry turned his crumpled gaze towards her. 'Miss Maguire?'

'I just wondered if, um… if we can talk to the punters.'

To her relief, Sir Gerry seemed amused rather than angry at her question. 'Talk all you like, lass. Don't expect to get any sense out of them, though!' He gave a wheezing chuckle, and the Trainees joined in, politely. 'Rule One – the customer doesn't know what they want. It's up to you to tell them!' Sir Gerry narrowed his eyes at them. 'Any more questions?'

The Trainees exchanged glances.

'Then get to work!' exclaimed Sir Gerry, and waved his hands to usher them away.

As Kate headed along the corridor with the others, she remembered the icy glare of Miss Devonshire's eyes again, and felt a shiver up her spine. Just like that time, not so long ago, when she'd been 'invited' to the school office to discuss her truancy. It was an uncomfortable echo, and the feeling of unease followed her back down the corridor and into the lift.

'Hold on, Reece! Just… hold on!' Chantelle Stanford, alarmed, looked over her shoulder at her brother. Reece was gripping the seat and looking rather green as the Doomcastle train lurched into a dimly lit tunnel, from which an icy draught emerged like a winter wind.

The Doctor was peering through his glasses at the construction of the tunnel. 'Don't like the look of those pit-props,' he said. 'Need to get a man in. Wonder when they were last inspected?'

'That ain't helping!' snarled Chantelle.

The Doctor looked abashed. 'Sorry.'

The rickety train lurched as it rounded a corner. That second there was a screech like the rending of metal mixed with a banshee howl, and an unearthly, yellowish-green glow suffused the carriage.

The children, and some of the adults, screamed at the clattering, skeletal figure which had reared up in front of them out of the cobweb-bedecked darkness, and which was now leering over the top of the train as if to devour the passengers. There was a strong smell of burning sulphur.

The Doctor peered up at it, grinning. 'Ohhhh, this is brilliant. *Brilliant*.' He shook his head in wonder. 'I've not seen one this good since Disneyland. Or was it the Golden Mile?'

The train hooted, belched steam, and began to pick up speed, leaving the glowing ghoul behind.

'Is it supposed to be going this fast?' Reece complained.

'Oh, for goodness' sake, Reece,' said his mum, Tricia, from

across the aisle, who was already on her third packet of crisps since starting the journey ten minutes earlier. She rolled her eyes at the Doctor. 'He gets motion sickness just by walking. Doesn't he, Derek?' she added to her boyfriend.

Derek gave an apologetic smile and said nothing.

'Derek can't speak,' said Tricia Stanford to the Doctor, by way of explanation. 'His doctor's told him to rest his voice for two weeks. Says it'll help his stress. God knows how.'

The Doctor gave a non-committal 'Aahhh' in their general direction.

The train slammed round at a sharp angle, descending through some quite convincing, curtain-like cobwebs. Glistening spiders the size of cats clicked and scuttled in the slimy, stony darkness above the passengers' heads.

The Doctor peered at the arachnids through a pair of opera glasses which he'd produced from his jacket pocket. 'Oh, very clever. Very advanced animatronics for the time. They almost look real.' He shook his head. 'Amazing what they can do with special effects these days.'

The ghost train hooted again. It was heading down an incline now, descending into the chilly heart of the Doomcastle.

The Doctor raised his eyebrows at the wild lurches the train was giving. 'The speed this thing's going...' he muttered to himself. 'The brakes must be the size of Belgium!' He knew the ride was meant to be exciting, but from the start something about it had left him wondering if it was meant to be taken at quite such a pace.

Armoured figures lined the slippery walls, heads swivelling from side to side, while giant bats swirled over the roof of the carriage.

'Their slime's not much good,' complained Chantelle. 'They had better slime at Ghostland Heights. Mind you, that was just CGI. It looked well unconvincing.'

The Doctor pulled a face. 'Aw, well. Seen one lot of slime, you've seen them all, really. And I've seen quite a bit. Probably too much.'

The train hooted again, and was thundering down an incline, swerving alarmingly at each corner, rattling and juddering. Screams and moans emanated from hidden speakers.

As if to confirm the Doctor's suspicions, several passengers were looking alarmed now and hanging on to their seats. Tricia, looking red and flushed, had dropped her crisps.

A cackling witch popped from a fiery cauldron, but they barely had time to see it, such was the speed at which the train was going.

The Doctor, suddenly making a decision, reached out of his side of the train and grabbed hold of the witch's broomstick. 'I'll bring it back!' he shouted, and leapt to his feet and, wobbling as the train hurtled and bumped, tried to make his way to the front of the carriage and the driver.

'What are you doing?' snapped Chantelle.

'Don't tell anyone,' said the Doctor breathlessly, 'but I think this thing is out of control.'

'What are you gonna do?'

He looked surprised. 'I'm not quite sure yet.' He looked down at the broomstick and gripped it firmly. 'Right. Va-va-broom!' The Doctor leapt to the front of the train, past the alarmed families. 'Ladies and gentlemen,' he said, struggling to keep his balance. 'Minor technical fault. Please stay in your seats while we sort it out.'

He leapt over the gap into the locomotive and peered at the animatronic driver. Its hands were gripping the controls hard, the rigid, grinning cartoon face beneath the blue hat turning from side to side under the control of some kind of motor.

The Doctor had calculated, by comparing the speed of the train with the sound of the engine and the angle of the incline, that it wasn't supposed to be going this fast. And now they were thundering into the bowels of the Doomcastle so fast that the train risked coming off the rails altogether.

He leaned down, flipped open a panel on the instrument board, pulled out two wires and touched them together. There was a haze of blue, followed by a screech of brakes, and the train began to judder and lose velocity. Fountains of orange sparks flew up in the darkness, steam engulfed the cabin and the smell of hot metal filled the dark air. People screamed. Something went *pop* very loudly, like a cracker.

The Doctor stood up, hands pushing his hair back so that it stood up in mad spikes. 'Well, I did *something*,' he muttered.

The engine had stopped, but, thanks to the slight downward incline of the track, the train was still rolling slowly forwards. The driver's motorised head swung round and it appeared to glare straight at the Doctor with its impassive, cartoon-grin face.

'Blimey,' the Doctor muttered. 'Where's the Fat Controller when you need him?'

He jumped out onto the track and jammed the broomstick diagonally between the locomotive and the stone wall. To his amazement and delight, it held firm, jamming the train so that it was, at least for the moment, motionless.

The Doctor peered at the broomstick interestedly. 'So what are you made of? Not wood, that's for sure...' He jumped up. 'No time. *People.*' He leapt back into the carriage and addressed the shaken-looking passengers. 'Right, sorry about that. Quick, er, health and safety inspection. If you all wouldn't mind getting off and walking to the end of the tunnel? It's not far.'

Grumbling, looking at each other in incomprehension and shrugging, people eventually began collecting their bags and moving.

The Doctor ushered them off the train with a smile. 'Come on, that's it. Nice and quick, please. *Pronto, pronto.* Thank you very much. Off, please. *Aussteigen.*'

'Is this all part of it?' asked Tricia, as she tottered uncertainly down from the train in her leopard-skin high heels. 'I said to Derek, I bet this is all part of it.'

The Doctor thought they'd better not go into that right now. 'Just keep moving, please. Do ensure you have all your belongings with you, and, er, all that sort of thing... Reece, Reece!' He slapped the boy on the shoulder. 'Managed not to vomit. Good man. Keep it up. I mean, um, keep it down. You know what I mean.'

As soon as most people were off the train, the Doctor – glancing to check that the broom was still holding it in place – jumped back up onto the locomotive and peered closely at the driver.

'Now, then, let's take a look at you, matey.' The Doctor loosened the driver's blue plastic cap with his sonic screwdriver and lifted it off, revealing the gleaming silver dome of the head beneath. He tapped it. The surface looked like metal, but felt softer, shinier. The Doctor rubbed it, licked the end of his finger and pulled a face. 'Interesting. All right.'

He hopped out of the train and scrambled down to meet

the passengers, who had assembled, nervously, in the greenish light by one of the train junctions, watched over by a black-armoured knight.

'Right, then,' said the Doctor breezily, and clapped his hands. 'Sorry about the impromptu ending. Shall we see what we can find in the Doomcastle?' He folded his arms. 'D'you know, I love saying that. *Doooom*-castle. You pretty much know what you're going to get with that, don't you?'

'You don't work here,' said Chantelle. She had her arms folded and was chewing gum, looking at the Doctor with threatening insolence.

'Sorry?' The Doctor looked at her, wide-eyed.

'You've got no more idea what's going on than the rest of us, have you? Why don't we just wait here for the mechanics to arrive, or whatever?'

'Weeeell, because then you'll have missed your chance to have a bit of an exploration. You're up for a bit of an exploration, aren't you?'

Several of the small children cheered. Their parents started to look visibly more relieved, obviously convinced that this was all part of Hyperville's package of attractions.

'OK, then!' said the Doctor cheerfully. 'Off we go!'

They trooped off into the torch-lit passage, heading for the wooden doors at the end.

As the last of the passengers left the junction, the suit of armour creaked. Then, slowly, the shiny black visor turned towards the group, and watched them go.

In his chair, Max Carson mopped his sweating brow. He'd had a very trying couple of days, and he suspected things were about to get worse.

Max leaned forward, looking at one of the hundreds of monitor screens in front of him.

'Magnify him,' he murmured.

The high-definition CCTV image flipped out, filling his own personal viewscreen. The image closed in on the Doctor's face as he smiled and chatted with the passengers, gesturing upwards like a tour guide.

Car-ssssson...

'Fascinating,' said Max. He licked his lips. He cupped a hand to his ear as if receiving a message through an earpiece. 'Our friend with the capacity to override the ticketing system obviously fancies he has a future in the tourism industry. Perhaps we should tell Sir Gerry. Or, er, maybe Butlin's.'

There was a ripple of polite laughter among the operatives in the control room. Everyone knew it was a good idea to find Mr Carson's quips amusing.

Caaaaar-ssson!

'Keep a fix on him,' said Max sternly, cupping his ear again. 'I want to know what he does.'

He flicked a control on his chair, and the floor swallowed him up once more. He descended through a glass tube, carried on his personal platform.

Car-ssson! Report!

'I'm on my way,' he said, seemingly to nobody. 'Just... dealing with a little... local restlessness.'

Max Carson's personal lift, unseen by anyone, descended further into the tube – down, down, past the shopping levels and the casino levels, deep down into the bowels of Hyperville.

Where something was waiting for him.

***

Kate was being proactive.

Rather than retreating to her room with Sir Gerry's documents, as her fellow Trainees had done, she had got out into Hyperville straight away, her Access All Areas badge pinned to her lapel, her Hypercard in her pocket.

She'd never believed in sitting and reading rules – she wanted to be out there finding out how it all worked. Ask questions, take notes. Surely that was what it was all about.

And that was what she needed to do. For her own purposes.

After two hours chatting to endless store managers and security officers, Kate felt she'd earned herself a coffee and, as she paid for it at a stall off Europa Plaza, she became aware of a large crowd gathering by the giant, blue Waterwall.

'What's going on?' Kate asked the stallholder.

'Shaneeqi,' said the man with a grin. 'Doing her promo signing.'

Kate tingled with excitement. So – one of the world's biggest pop stars was right here in Europa Plaza and she hadn't been aware. She glanced nervously back at the stallholder as she sipped her coffee. Maybe he was watching? Maybe they were all watching, all primed to report back to Sir Gerry on who was asking the most sensible questions, who was being the busiest?

A curved white table was set up with copies of Shaneeqi's silver-jacketed autobiography, *Sound Life*. Some of the crowd were clutching their own copies, while others held CDs.

Kate was prepared to shoulder her way to the front of the excitable crowd, but she found the black-capped security men ready to hold people back for her. She smiled and nodded at them. Only some of them nodded back. Fifty metres above her, an Oculator bobbed in the air; she could see it, a black dot against the backdrop of the Waterwall. She knew there were at least ten of them, now. She remembered showing that school friend – Lisa, was it? – the very first one, that day they skipped school together in Year 11. She knew from her reading that Hyperville still had the exclusive contract for those floating surveillance devices, even though other organisations were begging to be allowed access to them. Not for the first time, Kate wondered why somewhere like Hyperville seemed to need so much security. Surely it wasn't an obvious terrorist target in the way a military or scientific installation was?

A mere nod got Kate through to the backstage area, which was more cramped than she'd thought it would be. There was the young megastar, easily recognisable – crop-top, silver hotpants, spiky crimson hair and terracotta fake-tan – drinking bottled water with her entourage. Shaneeqi was meant to be a health freak, Kate knew. It was rumoured she ate mainly vegetables and drank nothing but water. As Kate approached the group, she saw the girl's heavily made-up face turn towards her. She realised she was smaller and bonier in real life than she looked on the TV.

Kate extended a hand, her heart pounding. 'Hi, Shaneeqi? Just wanted to say hello. I'm Kate Maguire, Sir Gerry's assistant.' It was a brave bluff, but she carried it off. Shaneeqi grinned, shook her hand. The young star's hand was cold, Kate noticed, but her grip was firm.

'All right,' she said in her casual South London voice.

'Umm…' Kate shrugged, grinned. 'Everything OK?'

Shaneeqi took a cautious bite of one of the cauliflower-sticks on the buffet arranged for her. 'Are these organic, darlin'?' she asked. 'I said I wanted organic.'

'One hundred per cent organic, I assure you,' said Kate smoothly, not having the faintest idea if that was true or not. She could see the entourage eyeing her up – a couple of young men in suits with T-shirts, two muscular guys in baseball gear and a woman in shades who appeared to have silvery-white hair down to her waist. 'Is Paul joining you?'

The 23-year-old pop-star had caused a stir recently by marrying England football heart-throb Paul Kendrick, who played in Italy for most of the year. A golden showbiz couple, they were rarely out of the magazines Kate read.

'He's flying in,' said Shaneeqi. She looked at Kate as if she was stupid. 'From Milan? His helicopter's, like, bringing him from Heathrow.'

Kate smiled. 'Of course. Yes.' She nodded at the additional piles of the autobiography beside the buffet. 'Book doing well?'

Shaneeqi shrugged. 'Think so. Don't really know.'

'How long did it take you to write?' Kate asked.

Shaneeqi laughed. 'Oh, I dunno. I just spouted into a microphone and some journalist bloke wrote it all down.' She peered at Kate's badge again. 'The Zone's all ready, then, darlin'? Cause I've not seen it, yet.'

'The Zone. The Zone! Yes, of course, yes. The Zone is fine. All clear. All ready.' Kate realised that she was babbling, and tried to maintain her serene grin. 'Umm… tell me about what you… are looking forward to most about it.'

'Between you and me,' said Shaneeqi, 'I dunno if I'm going to like it. I mean – a whole Zone of the FunGlobe dedicated to *meeee*!' She gasped, put her hand to her chest in mock-horror. 'I mean, I know I'm, like, fabulous, but this is just amazing.'

'Amazing,' agreed Kate.

So amazing, she thought, that she didn't even know about it. She was beginning to understand Sir Gerry's strategy of keeping them all in a hotel for two months with no media access. It put them at a disadvantage – even those who'd been to Hyperville as customers before. They still had to get up to speed with the latest developments in the place.

'Well,' said Kate, 'any problems, anything you need, just ask for me, OK? Kate Maguire.' She tapped her ID badge with her index finger.

'Sure. No, we're fine. Just waiting for the nod that Paul's landed on the helipad, and we'll be off.'

'I can find out how long he'll be for you,' offered Kate.

'Oh, would you? Darlin', that'd be *great*.' Shaneeqi gave her a broad, dazzling smile, as fake as her tan.

Kate smiled as she put the phone to her ear, and turned away so that Shaneeqi couldn't see her wincing. 'This'll be fun,' she muttered.

Using his sonic screwdriver as an additional light source, the Doctor led the group of tourists through the dark, cobwebbed Hall of the Doomcastle.

It was bitingly cold, and sound effects of chilly wind played in the background, adding to the atmosphere. Candles burned in candelabras – fake flames, the Doctor imagined – while grim-faced subjects in Victorian dress looked down on them from vast, golden-framed portraits. Suits of armour lined the walls, and the fluttering of bats in the rafters could be heard.

Tricia Stanford shivered and pulled her fur coat more tightly around her. 'I don't like this. It's like that, whassit, Rockyville Horror or whatever it's called. Isn't it, Derek?'

Derek smiled tightly and nodded.

'Oh, come on, this is great!' said the Doctor with relish, craning his neck and shining his light into the Hall's darkest recesses. 'Very Gothic. The most Gothic castle in Gothictown, Gothicland.' He paused, looked back down. 'There's only one thing missing, really.'

On cue, a connecting door creaked open, slamming against the wall, and an icy draught whipped through the Hall. Shattering, discordant organ music echoed through the rafters. Tricia screamed. Chantelle and Reece clung together, while several of the smaller children shrieked or whimpered and hid behind their parents.

From the doorway, a tall, dark figure stalked – black-cloaked, talon-like fingernails outstretched, eyes bright green under a shining cap of black hair. The figure opened its mouth, showing a perfect set of white fangs.

The Doctor folded his arms and smiled. 'That's what was missing.' He put his head on one side, sizing the vampire up. 'Ohhh, I'm impressed. Advanced animatronics. These things normally just sort of… stand there and… swivel their heads a bit.' The Doctor bobbed his own head from side to side as if to illustrate the point. 'I wonder…'

The organ music ramped up a semitone or two.

'Yeah, yeah, all right!' The Doctor rolled his eyes, raised his voice so that he was addressing the rafters. 'Hammer the point home, why don't you? Blimey, you people like to frighten the kids. You'll be breeding a nation of bedwetters.'

The vampire shuffled forward, its shiny plastic face swivelling towards the group of tourists, eyes shining with an unearthly glow.

The Doctor ducked behind the animatronic vampire, flipped his sonic screwdriver up towards it. 'Open wide, sunshine. Ever thought you might be getting a bit long in the – no, no, I refuse to do that joke. Even for you lot.'

He applied his sonic screwdriver to the artificial vampire's ear, and the effect was immediate. It shrieked – or possibly made a whining sound caused by the grinding of some internal mechanism – and the head spun round a full circle before slumping forward. Its arms hung limply in front of it, making it look like a puppet with the strings loosened.

The Doctor grinned. 'There we are.' He raised his eyebrows at the crowd. 'You know, vampires… they're really *rubbish*, aren't they? I mean there are, what, six… *seven* ways to kill them?'

'Doctor—' Chantelle began.

'And one of those involves waving a key ingredient of Italian cuisine in their faces. I mean, that's *got* to be rubbish.'

Chantelle folded her arms. 'Doctor,' she said patiently. 'Mate. Seriously. Is there a way we can get out of here?'

'Yes. Sorry. Um…' The Doctor looked around. 'Maybe we can get out a way they don't intend us to, eh? And I can get round to reporting that fault.' He ushered them through the door from which the vampire had emerged. 'Come on, perfectly safe now. Head up the stairs, keep going till you get to the top. Logic tells me that's the emergency exit. Although if you see a big green sign at the top marked "Emergency Exit", that might be even better than logic.'

Reece, who was looking a little less green now, poked the Doctor in the ribs. 'Fangs a lot,' he said. 'Geddit? *Fangs* a lot.'

The Doctor rolled his eyes. 'There's always one.'

Chantelle pushed her brother forward. 'Come on. Let's go and check out the SherwoodZone.' She nodded at the Doctor. 'Thanks for your help, mister. Sorry I was rude to you.'

The Doctor looked up from examining the vampire. 'Were you? I didn't really notice.'

When they had all gone, the Doctor pulled a pair of tweezers and a specimen jar from his pocket, gently eased one of the shiny white fangs out of the vampire's mouth and popped it into the jar.

'Just borrowing that,' he said quietly. 'Don't worry.'

He popped the jar into his pocket and turned to go.

And then the two suits of armour either side of the door stepped forward, halberds raised in both hands, and blocked his way.

'Oh!' said the Doctor. 'Right. Um.' He swallowed hard. 'No through road. Right, well… Back the way I came, then.'

He turned to head back towards the main doors of the Hall – and, as he did so, they flew open with a theatrical thunderclap and another gust of cold wind.

Two witches were hovering there, about a metre off the ground, gripping their broomsticks in gnarled yellow hands. Their black capes were streaming in the wind and their wizened green faces were lowered towards him, while thin-lipped mouths leered, showing yellow teeth.

The Doctor's eyes opened in astonishment. 'Gas-jet levitation? You shouldn't have the technology for *that*.'

As if to prove him wrong, the witches lifted slowly on their broomsticks, their eyes glowing yellow.

They paused for a second, floating in mid air. Then they swooped towards the Doctor.

THREE

'I thought we agreed!' Max Carson's voice was sharp and angry in the vast, underground space. His footsteps echoed as he paced up and down in the vast, metallic blackness. His breath misted in the cold air. Harsh green light bathed him and Miss Devonshire.

Sprawled in a leather swivel-chair, Miss Devonshire shrugged. 'She was a danger. She needed to be eliminated, Max.'

Max Carson shook his head. 'I don't like it. *Killing!* That was never part of it.' He glared up at her angrily. 'It's n-not what I agreed to!'

Miss Devonshire shrugged and smiled. 'You're a part of it now, Max. Whether you like it or not.'

'That j-j-journalist woman. People will ask questions. Her friends, her family.' Max shivered, flapping his arms to keep warm. Why, he thought, hadn't he brought a coat?

'By then, it will be too late!'

'What have you done with her?'

Miss Devonshire tweaked her gold watch and a previously invisible hologram screen blossomed into life on the metallic wall. It showed a row of shop-window dummies, their plastic faces jet-black and glossy, their hair sculpted.

Max shuddered. 'I don't really care for those things,' he said, trying to stop his teeth from chattering.

'Max, Max, Max!' She gave him a broad, tight-lipped smile. He really didn't like Miss Devonshire's red-lipsticked smiles. They reminded him of a clown. 'You are talking about the foot-soldiers of my employers. Show a little respect!' She chuckled. 'Look closely,' she said, as the image panned across the department store.

Max peered at the screen. He wondered for a minute what he was supposed to be looking for. Then he blinked.

'No,' he said.

'Oh, yes.'

'But… how?'

'Plastinol-2. You should know, Max, you of all people. You helped us to develop it.'

'But you said Plastinol-2 was going to be a *good* thing! That it would help the human race progress!'

'Did I?' Miss Devonshire made a dismissive *tchah* sound. 'You need to know nothing, Max, except that you, as promised, will be rewarded handsomely at the end of this. Handsomely enough to retire to Barbados. No…' She waved a hand. 'Go back out there and get on with doing what you do best. Be all butch and sinister.' She growled at him. 'I love it when you do that.'

For a moment, Max Carson bristled with anger. Then he had a last look at the hologram screen, where he could see the last mannequin in the display picked out in sculpted, glossy waves of dark plastic – the mannequin with the unmistakable face of Andrea Watkins.

Then he nodded grimly, turned on his heel and left.

'Oh, Max,' Miss Devonshire called after him. 'You do *flounce* so wonderfully.'

Maintenance Worker Jeff Smethwick was beginning to think he and Bob got all the dull jobs.

Bob, proudly bald and in his sixties, was the oldest man employed on the Hyperville service team, while Jeff was the fresh-faced youngster, still within his probationary period. Bob didn't drink or smoke and worked out at the gym, and often made Jeff feel like the old one.

Jeff, as he followed his experienced colleague through the tunnel, torch held at shoulder-height, was nervous – he'd never liked tunnels.

He'd taken this job because he'd hated working in a factory, and he'd been assured he'd be assigned to the SherwoodZone, as close to the open air as it was possible to be without actually being outside.

Deep in his heart, he really wanted to be a park ranger. But, so far, the job had seemed to involve a lot of tunnels, cupboards, lift shafts and other cramped spaces.

'I'm telling you,' Bob was saying, as they made their way along the dingy maintenance tunnel, 'you can't put ham and cheese together. It isn't natural. Got to be one or the other.'

Jeff grinned. It was a familiar argument. 'All right, Bob. I'm sure the world's going to fall apart because I've got an unconventional sandwich filling. Where do you stand on pickle? Bob?'

Bob had stopped, and swung round to face back down the service tunnel. 'I thought I heard something,' he said, shining his torch into the dark recesses.

'Probably the rats,' Jeff suggested nervously.

Bob gave a humourless smile. 'Rats, in Hyperville? Mr Carson would have kittens.'

'Which would actually be quite a good idea,' said Jeff, aware that he was gabbling now to cover up his own nervousness. 'You know. Cats. Send them into the tunnels to—'

'Sssh!' Bob held up a hand. 'There it is again! Didn't you hear it?' He activated the slim, orange wrist-radio which all the maintenance staff wore. 'I'm going to give Control a call.'

'I didn't hear anything,' Jeff whispered.

'Quiet, lad.' A hiss of static echoed through the tunnel, and Bob swore quietly, thumping the radio with the palm of his hand. 'Blasted things! The damn batteries are always playing up.' He cleared his throat. 'Wait here,' he said to Jeff, and set off back the way they had come.

Jeff shivered. He saw Bob's silhouette recede into the darkness, and saw the wobbling aura of the torch-light disappearing round the corner. He paced up and down to stop himself from getting nervous. They weren't supposed to be left on their own, he thought worriedly. Not down here. Always work in pairs, that was the mantra.

'Bob?' he called. 'Bob?'

He could still just about see the glimmering light from Bob's torch from round the corner.

His heart racing, the sweat making his armpits clammy, Jeff turned in a full circle, desperately trying to keep his torch on all parts of the tunnel at once. 'Bob, are you there?' he called.

He was sure he could hear something now. Further up the tunnel, where they hadn't been yet. Where was the hatch to the SherwoodZone? Jeff checked the maintenance-point number on the wall – 247. Only three checkpoints away from the hatch, so not that far – could be one of the exhibits playing up, he reasoned, trying to calm himself with logical thoughts. Or maybe it was one of the punters playing silly beggars.

'Who's up there?' he called. 'Anyone?'

For a second, Jeff was sure he caught a shape in the blaze of his torch, further into the tunnel near Maintenance Checkpoint 248. He jumped, and felt his heart pounding faster.

'Bob!' he called over his shoulder. 'Bob, you there?'

Jeff began to back up in the tunnel, his hand shaking as it held the torch.

'*Bob!*' he shouted.

Jeff walked backwards, training his flashlight on the place in the shadows where he had seen the figure.

And a second later, he crashed straight into something.

He gasped, jumping back – shining his torch up into the shiny, bald head of his colleague.

Jeff breathed a huge sigh of relief.

'All right, lad,' Bob said gruffly. 'Don't go getting afraid of your own shadow, now.' He clapped a hand on Jeff's shoulder and jerked a thumb back down the corridor. 'There were a loose covering back there. Flapping in the draught. I fixed it back.'

Jeff sensed relief coursing through his body, making him feel weak but also strangely re-energised. 'Can we get the job done and get out of here, mate? I don't like these places.'

'Come on, lad,' said Bob, smiling. He led the way down the tunnel towards Checkpoint 248, and then stopped short. 'Wait,' he said.

Bob held his torch steady and shone it into the shadows ahead of them.

Jeff's jaw dropped.

Two dark figures stood there. They looked like ordinary people – a man and a woman, dressed smartly. Jeff thought, for a moment, that they looked bizarrely like guests at a wedding. The man wore a purple necktie with a matching light-purple shirt and a steely grey suit. The woman had a jacket and skirt in silver-grey, set off by a purple corsage and a bright, sparkly mauve fascinator in her hair. Jeff couldn't make out their faces in the gloom – they seemed strangely featureless, like robbers in stocking-masks.

'You folks shouldn't be down here,' said Bob sharply. 'What are you up to?'

The interlopers lifted their arms, pointing at Bob and Jeff as if accusing them of something.

The maintenance men looked at each other in puzzlement.

Bob shook his head. 'I don't like this,' he said. 'Let's get back to 247. Seal this off and report it to Mr Carson.'

Jeff nodded. They turned to make a break for it – and found their retreat blocked by another figure.

This one was different.

For a start, it was smaller – only the size of a child. Its burnished, plastic face reflected the light of the torches, and its eyes seemed to glow a dull red in the dimness.

As the figure stepped forward, Jeff saw to his astonishment that it looked like a small girl, dressed in bright red trousers and a white-and-pink striped jumper. But its face – its face was –

The girl cackled, and lifted her arm to point at the two men.

Her eyes glowed red.

A second later, there was a bright crimson flash in the dimness, followed by a billow of pink smoke.

Two torches dropped to the floor and rolled to the edge of the maintenance tunnel.

Captain Tess Tilbrook stood on the helipad on the roof of the ShopZone, her cropped grey hair unruffled by the wind. She was flanked by two impassive, black-uniformed guards armed with sub-machine guns.

Just a few years earlier, Tess thought, it would have been impossible for Sir Gerry to run the place like this. Armed guards, CCTV everywhere, ID mapping of every customer's preferences through the Hypercards... These days, with everything that had happened in the world, it was almost expected. It would seem strange if the Chief Exec didn't demand extra monitoring and protection for his customers.

Tess wasn't sure she liked the idea very much. But Head of Security at Hyperville was a very well-paid job. She was bringing up two teenage sons on her own, and employment was an increasingly precarious thing to have in this day and age.

What Sir Gerry and the Corporation paid her enabled her to meet the mortgage on a house in a very nice part of town, to have two holidays a year with her sons, and to indulge her hobbies of canoeing and abseiling every weekend. On her last canoeing trip she'd met Kevin, a divorced bloke with nice eyes who'd asked her out for a drink. They were going on their second date this weekend.

A shadow fell over the helipad, and Tess looked up, shading her eyes. 'Look out, lads,' she muttered. 'Here he comes.'

The big, black shape of the helicopter began to descend, the accompanying wind whipping at their uniforms. Almost as soon as it touched down, he emerged, ducking under the rotor-blades – the immaculate figure of Paul Kendrick.

Tess couldn't help a feeling of pride as she saw England's national hero striding towards her in his Armani suit and Police shades. With his gleaming white teeth and spiky blond hair, Kendrick was football's pin-up boy, but he was still the best player England had produced in the last twenty years. He'd seemed to emerge from nowhere – even Tess, who followed football with her boys, had been surprised. Within two years he was captaining England, and at the Euro 2012 semi-final against Spain he'd put the winning goal into the back of the net. It was only Kendrick's absence through injury, it was generally agreed, which had prevented England from taking the trophy in the final against Portugal.

Paul Kendrick grinned, offering her his hand. He had a very firm grip, Tess noticed. 'All right,' he said affably. He gave her a big, shiny grin, but she couldn't read his eyes behind his mirror-lenses.

'Captain Tess Tilbrook, head of security. Did you have a good trip, Mr Kendrick?'

'Yeah. Not bad. Call me Paul.' He buttoned his jacket, as if nervous, and looked around the helipad. 'Sir Gerry not here?'

Tess smiled. 'Sir Gerry and Mr Carson have been delayed on business matters, I'm afraid. But if you'd like to come with me? Shaneeqi's done her warm-up signing in the Plaza, and we're having the reception tonight in the Aura Casino.'

'Nice one,' said Paul Kendrick.

A man of few words, thought Tess. He was never especially loquacious in interviews. It was something of a standing joke that his answers were always the standard footballer clichés, where he assured reporters that the boys had done good and it had been a game of two halves.

But Tess couldn't shake the idea that he had something on his mind today. She was going to wonder what it was, but then remembered that she wasn't paid to wonder.

'Come this way,' she said, and she and the guards led the young England captain across the helipad towards the lift.

'Mr Carson?'

Max spun round in his chair, raising an eyebrow. It was one of the younger Trainees, he noted, striding with false confidence across the gantry that connected his chair-platform to the outer door. She stood there, hands clasped confidently in front of her, but betraying her nervousness by swivelling on one heel.

'Yes?' said Max with a sigh. He was still disconcerted by his meeting with Miss Devonshire, and the last thing he wanted now was another problem.

'Kate Maguire from the Trainees, Mr Carson.' She smiled.

'Yes, yes, I remember you. Get to the point.'

Her smile vanished. 'Um. Oh, sorry. Mr Kendrick's just arriving. Thought I'd let you know.'

'Mr Kendrick?'

'Yes, ah, Shaneeqi's husband. The footballer. You know. Goldenball Paul, Kicker Kendrick, last-minute penalty in Euro 2012. Did you watch that? It was brilliant.'

Max Carson spread his hands. 'Why, *precisely*, are you telling me this?'

Kate blushed. 'I'm sorry, sir. I thought you'd find the information interesting.'

Max gestured languidly around him at the curved wall with its honeycomb of CCTV screens. 'Let me tell you some information *you* will find interesting, Miss Maguire. From here, I see everything, OK? I'm the Director of Operations. I *know* what's going on in Hyperville. The cameras, the Oculators, the sound-bugs – everything keeps me informed. If somebody sneezes, Max Carson knows about it.' He gave her a brief, dazzling smile. 'Clear?'

Kate looked abashed. 'Clear, sir. Sorry, sir.' Then she frowned and lowered her glasses. 'What's going on there?' she asked, pointing at one of the screens near the top left of the display.

Max Carson whirled round. 'Enlarge and focus!' he ordered.

The plasma screen in front of him leapt into life. It was that idiotic man from before, Max saw – the one who had interfered with the ticket machine. He appeared to be in the Hall of the Doomcastle Sector, backing slowly away from two of the Witch-bots, while two of the Knight-bots stalked towards him from behind.

Max clenched his fists. 'I think it's about time we had a word with our friend.'

'Who is he?' asked Kate curiously, leaning forward.

It was almost, thought Max for a second, as if she recognised him.

'A criminal,' said Max dismissively. 'One with some... unusual technology.'

He remembered that Sir Gerry had given instructions for the Trainees to be allowed to go anywhere they liked and ask any questions they wanted. And Sir Gerry, for the moment, was in charge.

'It looks as if he's in danger,' said Kate worriedly.

Max smiled. 'Only as long as I allow him to be.'

You mean only as long as Miss Devonshire does, said the little voice inside his head.

'Ladies,' said the Doctor. 'I hate to seem rude, but I was *really* just about to leave.'

The two witches circled him on their broomsticks, pointed noses lowered at him and green eyes glowing. The Doctor was acutely aware of the two armoured knights behind him as well, clunking and clanking forward, both with halberds raised high above their shoulders.

'Thing is, I don't really know if you realise this, but this whole set-up is meant to scare kids. And I'm, well, about a thousand years old. Well, nine hundred and fifty… Well, nine hundred. Look, all right, I get mixed up. I lost a few birthdays somewhere.'

He backed slowly away, jumping onto the low table which ran the length of the Hall.

One of the knights suddenly swung its halberd into the table, missing the Doctor by centimetres. He jumped backwards. The witches rose, their blank, plastic Halloween-masks staring firmly ahead.

'You know, I think if you *reeeeeally* wanted to kill me you'd have done it by now.' He held his hands up. 'That's not an invitation or anything. Don't get me wrong.'

The witches hurtled forward.

They crashed into the Doctor, their broomsticks knocking into his shoulders and pitching him over onto the array of metal crockery on the table.

He rolled over, grabbed one of the candelabras and swung it up, just in time to deflect the blow of the second knight's halberd…

Kate, watching on the monitor, gasped.

'You've got to stop them! They're going to kill him!'

'My dear, they are simple mechanical devices for the entertainment of children. They can no more kill anybody than a salt-cellar could.'

Kate glared at Max. 'Stop them, Mr Carson!'

Max sighed, chuckling. 'Oh, all right.'

He reached out and punched a code into his control panel.

'Carson,' he said. 'Voice recognition. Circuit DC-47-B-98. Override.' He leaned back in his chair, spread his hands. 'There, Miss Maguire. Satisfied now?'

'Yes,' she said with a smile, folding her arms.

And she looked as if she meant it.

The Doctor had his hand above his head, ready to deflect whichever of the ghoulish apparitions decided to attack him next.

But in that very second, the lights in the witches' eyes went out and they dropped to the floor, as if their power of levitation had suddenly been lost. The two knights paused in mid-stride, halberds held in the air, once more like the motionless suits of armour they had been before.

The Doctor sat bolt upright, looked first one way and then

the other. 'And we were getting to know each other so well,' he said.

He put the candelabra down, flipped his glasses on and peered at the inert suit of armour. He tapped it gently, expecting a clang, but hearing instead a dull thud.

He wanted to take a closer look at his attackers. But something told him that enough was enough for the moment – and he had the vampire's tooth in the glass phial in his pocket. He bounded off the table and, with one quick look back, hurried up the stone spiral staircase which he hoped would lead him to the exit.

'You sure about this?' said Reece Stanford nervously to his sister as they stood in a mock-up of a rock-walled cave, waiting for some greenery-festooned doors to open.

Chantelle thumped him on the arm. 'Course. Don't be so stupid. You wouldn't rather be going shopping with Mum and Derek, would you?'

'Well… no,' admitted Reece. 'It's just that I feel a bit of a dork in this get-up.'

He gestured down at the ill-fitting green tunic, brown leggings and sandals which he had been given to wear in the entrance area of the SherwoodZone. Chantelle had come off better, having been fitted out in a smart Lincoln Green waistcoat and velvet trousers tucked into boots.

'All part of the fun, innit?' said Chantelle cheerfully. 'Ooh, look out – here we go!'

The doors swished open, and they stepped out into the forest.

Even the normally cynical Chantelle had to admit that she was quite impressed. She could tell the forest was artificial, enclosed within the great dome of the FunGlobe, but if you looked below the level of the trees it was pretty convincing – a throng of dense undergrowth, great canopies of verdant leaves drenched in what appeared to be sunlight, and a soft covering of leaf-strewn earth beneath their feet. There were mossy boulders, as well as crowds of bluebells, and other flowers which Chantelle did not recognise. The air was infused with an earthy, barky smell, and they could hear the sounds of gentle birdsong.

'Blimey,' murmured Reece. 'Sherwood Forest!'

'I was expecting a few tacky plastic trees,' said Chantelle in awe. 'And a Friar Tuck Burger Bar.'

'What was that?' Reece suddenly clutched her arm.

'What?'

'I saw something move. In the trees.'

'Dunno. A bird?'

'It was bigger than a bird,' said Reece crossly. 'Have you got anything to eat?'

She folded her arms and glared at him. 'Two hours ago you were feeling sick as a pig. Now all you're interested in is – wait a minute!' Chantelle ran across the forest clearing towards what she had seen. She beckoned Reece over. 'Look!'

It was an arrow, buried deep in the bark of the tree, pinning a fragment of parchment to the trunk. Chantelle removed the arrow and unrolled the parchment. It was marked with a rudimentary map, scrawled in black ink, with a big red X marked at one place near the centre.

'The Merry Men's hideout!' she said excitedly.

'You sure?' Reece glowered suspiciously. 'Could be a trap by the Sheriff of Whatsit. Norwich.'

Chantelle sighed and rolled her eyes. 'Nottingham, Reece.

It's *Nottingham*. You got any idea about geography?' She held a hand up. 'OK. Don't answer that. Come on.'

The two teenagers disappeared into the undergrowth, talking excitedly.

A second after they had gone, the dark, hooded figure which had been watching them from the shadows stepped out into the clearing. It nodded to itself, and gave a low, amused laugh.

Then, with green-booted feet making almost no sound on the soft earth, the figure slipped back into the cover of the forest.

'Attention. Attention. This is Hyperville. Please note that the Doomcastle is now closed to visitors for essential maintenance. Anyone holding an advance booking on their Hypercard may exchange it for other goods of an equal value at any Hyperville vending point. We apologise for the inconvenience. Shop. Dream. Relax.'

The Doctor, once he had made his way back through the vastness of the ShopZone, didn't take long to find the alcove beside the small gift shop where he had left the TARDIS. He strode round the corner with a big grin, ready to snap his fingers at precisely the right level of decibels and the correct frequency.

The grin froze on his face.

The TARDIS wasn't there.

Hearing movement behind him, the Doctor whirled round. Two armed security men stepped from the shadows, blocking off his retreat to Europa Plaza.

Another man – dark and goatee-bearded – appeared between them, smiling, hands clasped behind his back.

'Your… equipment has been, ah, impounded, sir,' he said. 'No parking permit.'

'Oh!' The Doctor backed towards the glass Emergency Exit doors behind him. 'Sorry about that. I did have one. Always losing these things. Sorry, um, I'm the Doctor, by the way.' He offered his hand.

'*The* Doctor. Just that? How interesting.' The man, who didn't offer a handshake back, raised an eyebrow. 'I'm Max Carson. Director of Operations.'

'Right. I suppose you know you've got rampaging exhibits on the loose in the Doomcastle? Not to mention a less-than-jolly train driver who very nearly killed a whole load of passengers?'

Max chuckled. 'Fanciful nonsense. Our operations are controlled by our Mark One Central Program, tested and protected to the absolute limit.'

'Mmmm. You say that, and yet you won't look me in the eye. You're a *rubbish* liar, Mr Carson, did you know that?'

'I don't know what you mean. Nothing can malfunction.'

'Try telling that to Witchy MacWitch and the Knight Twins. You've got yourself a few dodgy circuits down there. Well, that, or some *seriously* miffed members of the Horror Actors' Guild.' The Doctor scratched his ear and pulled an apologetic face.

Max rolled his eyes. 'I wonder,' he said smoothly, 'if you'd be good enough to join me for a meeting in my office, Doctor? Just to… discuss a couple of things?'

The Doctor, still rummaging in his pockets, looked pained. 'Oh? Meetings, nah, I don't really do meetings. Especially when there aren't any biscuits.'

'Doctor—'

'And don't you find it *really* irritating when someone's spent half an hour going on about the annual leave allocation and you've still got six items of Any Other Business to get through? I hate that. Don't you hate that?' In one movement, he had flipped his sonic screwdriver out and loosened the Emergency Exit doors behind him. Now, he kicked backwards and slipped through the gap. 'Send my apologies,' he said, and ducked into the staircase.

'Get after him!' snapped Max, and the two security men hurried to obey. Sighing, more in exasperation than anger, he flicked the attachment in his ear. 'Carson here. Got a wanderer in Europa, heading down towards the junction of Fifth Walk and Attenborough Boulevard. Get some units to apprehend, please. And try not to hurt him too much. I want to ask him some questions!'

At the foot of the stairs, the Doctor almost cannoned into a slim figure who stepped out in front of him. She was smartly dressed, aged about 20, with a feathered bob of black hair, an impudent snub-nose and smart glasses.

Coming to a breathless halt, the Doctor flipped his trusty psychic paper up in front of the woman.

The Doctor looked casual. 'Dr Johannes Schmidt. Structural engineering consultant.' He winced, tapped the breezeblock walls. 'Oooh, you've had some cowboys in here.'

The woman tapped the badge on her lapel. 'Kate Maguire. Management Trainee.' She tilted her head on one side. 'At least mine's not blank,' she added reprovingly.

The Doctor's jaw dropped. 'How did you… ?'

From above came the sound of clattering footsteps, as the security men hared down the stairs after the Doctor.

'Having a spot of bother?' said Kate. She opened a maintenance door to the side of the staircase. 'Get inside.'

The Doctor hesitated. 'How do I know I can trust you?'

'You don't. But I'm not carrying a gun. Unlike those guys.' She pointed up the stairs.

The Doctor swallowed hard. 'Good point, Kate Maguire. Well made. Come on, then.'

They ducked into the maintenance doorway, and Kate slammed it shut behind them.

Inside, they were in a low, tight tunnel lined with multicoloured cabling and grey junction boxes, lit by occasional orange panels along the walls. It smelt musty and hot.

'Let's move,' said Kate. 'Quickly.'

The Doctor grinned as they hurried along, ducking under the low, cable-lined ceiling. 'You sound like you've done this before. Why did you rescue me?'

'Because Mr Carson didn't like the look of you.'

'Yeah, there is that.'

'And Mr Carson's an idiot.'

'Ah, well, there's that too. You seem like a good judge of character, Kate Maguire.'

'*And* you looked as if you'd found something out that you shouldn't. You seem like a nose-poker to me. You a nose-poker?' She stopped, spun round, faced the Doctor with her arms folded and her eyebrows impishly raised.

'Um… well…' The Doctor didn't know what to say. 'I do sometimes make it my business to find things out.'

Kate beamed. 'Great! Me too. That's why I got myself on this Management scheme. I'm a trainee journalist.' She tapped the side of her nose. 'Strictly undercover. It's my project. Trying

to find out the real story behind Hyperville. It's kind of a...
lifelong obsession.'

'Rrrright. So you're not in it to work here, then?'

'Trust me, Doctor – I've no more got a business mind
than your real name is Johannes Schmidt. What *is* your real
name?'

'Just the Doctor.'

'What, just *The Doctor*?' Kate pulled a face. 'That's stupid.'

'No, no, it's—' The Doctor tutted, sighed and turned to face
her. 'Why? *Why* do people have such a problem with this? They
never ask Meat Loaf why he's named after an unfashionable
foodstuff, do they? Or tell J.D. Salinger, oh, no, you can't just
be J.D., you've got to have a *proper* first name?'

Kate held up a hand. 'OK, OK. Don't tell me. I'll try and
guess. It'll be our little bit of fun.' She shook her head. 'Didn't
realise it was such a touchy subject,' she muttered.

'I hope you like a challenge,' muttered the Doctor, as they
hurried on through the service ducts. 'By the way, um, Kate –
do you actually know where you're going?'

'Away from those guys,' said Kate. 'Can only be a good
thing, right?'

'Weeeelll...' The Doctor caught up with her, shaking his
head. 'Not necessarily. Depending on what's at the end.'
He grinned at her. 'Tell you what – while we look for a way
out, why don't you fill me in on what you know about
Hyperville...?'

'Ta-dah!' Tricia Stanford giggled and held up a silver-lamé
miniskirt against her none-too-pert bottom. 'Whaddya think,
Derek?'

Derek smiled weakly.

Endless miles of shops, stretching up above his head and away into the distance, were not really his idea of fun. Unfortunately, Tricia was in her element. Her annoying kids were off entertaining themselves in that SherwoodZone, which was a blessing, but he was still stuck here for the afternoon.

One of the security guards had said something about young Paul 'Goldenball' Kendrick being in the complex somewhere, which interested Derek far more than a lot of clothes shops. Granted, the young'un was no Bobby Moore, but it would still be worth trying to shake his hand.

'Oooh, how about this one?' Tricia asked, pulling what seemed like the thousandth item from the rack and holding it up against her voluptuous body. It was an all-in-one bodysuit consisting of a pink crushed-velvet top and leopard-skin leggings.

Derek shrugged and pulled a face. Gawd, he thought, that would look awful on a woman twenty years younger, let alone on her. What he really wanted to do was go and have a nice sit down and a cup of tea somewhere. Maybe even a scone.

Above him in the corner of the shop, the CCTV camera swivelled as if to admire Tricia's potential purchases. Derek scowled and folded his arms, cursing his throat ailment for the umpteenth time.

'No?' said Tricia disappointedly. She took another look at the garish item. 'Hmm, maybe it is a little *outré*, you know, *pour moi*.' She spotted something on a rack a few metres away. 'Don't go away, Derek,' she said. 'I've got the very thing.'

Derek groaned inwardly and looked at his watch.

Beside him, a family of glossy mannequins displayed the latest fashions – the father in a leather jacket and black jeans, the mother in a black shift-dress, wooden beads and a beret, and the toddler-dummy standing beneath them, displaying a striped jumper and cute pink trousers.

Derek shuddered. He didn't like shop dummies much at all, especially the sleek new sort. It was the way they looked nearly human, but not quite – the features smooth and unfinished, the sculpted hair, the eyes with no irises, the black plastic faces and limbs glossy and unblemished.

The shop was full of them, and so were the other superstores. They weren't just in the clothes sections, but in the shop windows and the other departments too, where they could be found brandishing kettles and saucepans, holding up books and even displaying helpful signs for customers.

He had to admit, he found them a bit creepy. And that went double for those modern ones with no heads.

'Ooooh, Derek,' said Tricia's voice from behind the multicoloured rack of clothes, 'how about this? Just the thing for drinks with the Hendry-Ellises. What do you think?' She poked her head round, and held up a hideous pink top covered with spangly spiderweb patterns.

Derek smiled weakly and gave her a thumbs-up. If he'd had a voice, he'd have said it was the kind of thing that Graham Norton bloke might have worn. Tricia disappeared again, in search of more prey.

When Derek looked back towards the dummies, the toddler-dummy's head was turned in the opposite direction.

Derek felt a chill, and his heart began to beat faster. He stepped slowly forward, leaned down towards the midget mannequin. Yes, its head was definitely looking down the aisles into the shop – and just a second ago, it had been looking out into the malls.

Someone must have moved it, Derek thought. They'd twisted the head round as they walked past.

He reached out and pressed his hand against the dummy's plastic cheek.

Oddly, it didn't feel as he had expected. He had thought it would feel cold, hard – instead it felt clammy and quite warm. Very unpleasant. Derek gave a grunt of displeasure and pulled his hand away. Horrible things, he thought.

And then the toddler-dummy's head turned round to look straight at him.

Derek jumped back in horror, staggering backwards into two young women.

'Oi!' one of them snapped. 'Watch where you're going, matey!'

'And keep your hands to yourself!' the other added.

Sweating, his heart pounding, Derek turned round, holding his hands up in a placatory gesture as the two girls stalked off, still looking over their shoulders and making disparaging comments towards him.

Derek peered down.

The toddler-dummy stared at him with its sightless eyes.

Tricia swept past him. 'Derek, what *are* you doing? There's nothing good here. Come on. We're going to Gladrags, and then if we can't find anything there we'll look in Henrik's.'

She paused at the big, open exit to the shop, as shoppers rushed past. She glared over her shoulder at her boyfriend. Derek was not ignoring her, but was backing cautiously away from the dummy.

'Derek, for goodness' sake! Come *on*!'

Derek finally broke his gaze from the dummy, and hurried off after Tricia towards the gleaming blue travelator-tubes.

Back in the shop, the toddler-dummy's eyes glowed a soft red.

On a soft-edged, oval screen, deep within the lowest basements of Hyperville, the face of Derek appeared, freeze-framed. Information poured onto a side-screen – data gained from scanning his iris and cross-matching with a national ID database.

'That one has seen too much,' said a mellifluous, female voice. 'Eliminate him. Eliminate him at the earliest opportunity!'

In the blackness at the edge of the solar system, a cluster of objects, each no bigger than a football, moved, keeping together in close formation. They were purplish-green in hue, roughly spherical but made up of flat, triangular sides. They pulsed gently in unison.

Their scarred, pitted surfaces had weathered all the debris which the cold reaches of space could throw at them.

They were relentless.

And coming closer.

FOUR

'Ten years' time,' Kate said, as she and the Doctor hurried through the dingy service-shaft, 'there'll be places like this all over the world. It started with the big shopping centres getting cinemas and saunas and stuff, and grew from there. They started realising people didn't come to them just for shopping, they came for *days out*. They'd do their shopping, get manicures and hair done, have a meal and go to the cinema. This is just the next generation.' She stopped, breathless. 'Doctor, are you *listening* to me?'

'Service ladder!' said the Doctor delightedly. He tapped the metal ladder and it gave a resounding ring. 'Seems sturdy enough.'

In the narrow tunnel, Kate hurried up behind him. They had been hurrying through the dimly lit labyrinth for what seemed like half an hour or more, she thought. This Doctor, whoever he was, seemed full of enthusiasm for tunnels.

It hadn't surprised Kate to see him, or to recognise him. It had taken her a minute or two to place the face – it had been four years, after all. But for now, she was keeping it to herself. Just as she was keeping the Hypercard to herself, tucked in the inside pocket of her pinstripe jacket. The one that the Doctor had given her, four years earlier.

'These stretch for miles,' she said. 'No idea where we might end up coming out. Could pop up in the middle of Shaneeqi's dressing room.'

'Aaaah, well.' The Doctor gave her a cheeky, sideways grin. 'Life needs an element of surprise, Kate. Come on!' He hopped onto the ladder and started climbing.

Kate sighed, and climbed up after the Doctor. She didn't really see what else she could do.

'So tell me about Sir Gerry. What's he doing, exactly?' the Doctor called down.

'He wants publicity,' Kate said. 'He advertised for young business-people to take part in an exercise. I think it's about seeing if we can find gaps in the organisation, make him more money. He probably thinks it's better than getting a team of consultants in.'

'And how did you get on board?' The Doctor, poking around in the ladder-shaft above him, seemed distracted.

'I found out about it. Got some fake credentials and references put together. My aunt's got a few useful contacts in the media.'

'Right…' The Doctor had found a metal hatch at an angle above the ladder, and was looking for an opening mechanism. 'Good stuff. Every thrusting young journalist needs a helpful aunt.'

'There's some big thing going on. Sir Gerry and Max Carson

– you met him earlier – they're planning a big switchover of all the Hyperville systems to a new centralised computer program.'

'Right. Interesting.'

'And that Miss Devonshire, I think she's involved somehow. She's there in the background, like an assistant, but I don't believe it for a moment. She's bankrolling it, I think.'

'And when's this happening?'

'Some time next week, supposedly. But there are always mutterings. Sir Gerry manipulates the mainstream media, but he's old-school. He forgets about the talkboards and the Bluetooth networks.'

'What are they saying?' asked the Doctor, as he applied his sonic screwdriver to the hatch.

'There's been a few… incidents. An electrician died a few weeks ago, in the WinterZone. Supposed to have been an accident – faulty connection they said. Then there was the WaterZone they just closed off.'

'Well, these things happen…' The Doctor pocketed his sonic screwdriver. 'But if you're suspicious already, then you do wonder.' He suddenly looked back down the shaft at Kate. 'Sorry – *whose* dressing room did you say?'

'Shaneeqi. She's here promoting her new Zone. There's a big cocktail reception bash tonight, in the Aura Casino.' Kate waited for the Doctor's reaction. 'Shaneeqi? No? Oh, come on, you must have heard of her. Biggest artist of the last five years. "Gimme Love Now"? "All That You Mean"? You *must* have heard "Don't Steal My Boyfriend, Girlfriend"? That was the vid-download Number One for nine weeks.'

'I've… been a bit out of touch,' said the Doctor awkwardly. 'How does it go again?'

Kate cleared her throat. 'I'm kind of hanging on a ladder here.'

'Oh, go on. Just a little burst.'

'Errm…' Kate, feeling embarrassed, bobbed her head from side to side, trying a vague impression of Shaneeqi's polished, mid-Atlantic intonation. 'It goes *"Don't steal my boyfriend, girlfriend/ She ain't my girlfriend, boyfriend/ Talk to the hand, listen to my band/ Na-na-na, yo, yo…"* There's kind of a few more na-na-nas. And a few more, er, yo-yos. That's… pretty much, like, the chorus.'

'Very good!' said the Doctor. 'You should go on *The X-Factor*. And, sorry, *how* many people bought this?'

'About five million,' admitted Kate. 'God, it's so sad that I *know* this,' she added to herself.

The Doctor shook his head. 'And she has a *Zone*? In Hyperville?'

'Well, yes, she will have,' said Kate. 'Sorry.'

The Doctor gave the hatch a shove and it squealed open, clanging as it hit the floor on the other side. 'Right, then,' he said, and hauled himself up onto a metal floor, reaching out to pull Kate up after him. A wall of cold hit Kate, and she shivered. The hatchway had brought them out in the middle of a snowy landscape, seemingly at night. Above them, remarkably realistic stars shimmered in a velvet-blue canopy of sky. Fir trees stretched into the distance, festooned with filigree spiderweb lights and dripping with glowing blue icicles. Kate and the Doctor's breath misted in the air.

Kate closed the hatch and straightened up beside the Doctor. 'I don't believe it,' she said, shaking with cold. The snow crunched beneath her feet, she noticed – it seemed real.

The Doctor beamed with boyish joy. 'Oooh, yes. Winter Wonderland! Ohh, this is *brilliant*! Like the SnowGlobe.' He looked at Kate. 'Sorry, somewhere else I went once.' He pulled an expandable telescope out of his pocket and surveyed the landscape. 'Aha! Look!'

Reluctantly, Kate took the telescope and trained it where the Doctor was pointing, down in the valley. The Hyperville train was puffing along, she saw, filled with laughing tourists in winter coats and hats. She shrugged, handed the telescope back to him.

'I hate Christmas,' she said through gritted teeth.

'Oh. Really?' The Doctor looked concerned. He frowned, peering down at her with genuine surprise on his face. 'No, *really*? What – all the logs on the fire and the gifts round the tree? And the carols and the lighty… light things and the mince pies?'

'Can't stand it,' said Kate grimly. 'It does my head in.' She wasn't going to go into any more details, not with this guy she hardly knew.

'Oh. Well, let's find a way out.' The Doctor pivoted on his heel. 'This way, I think.' He pointed to a spot between the trees.

'Listen!' Kate put a finger in the air. She was sure she had heard something – a silvery sound on the wind. A jangling noise.

The Doctor ran back to her side and smiled. 'Jingle bells, jingle bells!'

'I am seriously going to have to kill you if you keep loving this so much. How can you enjoy this?'

The Doctor raised his eyebrows at her. 'All right, all right, Ebenezer, keep your wig on. Anyway, why don't you do your job? Write down some notes about… profit and loss margins and… and all that.'

Kate folded her arms, annoyed. 'You haven't got a clue what you're talking about, have you?'

The jangling sound was getting louder. It was accompanied by a swishing – like the sound of skis, Kate thought, only louder, heavier.

A shape appeared over the snowy ridge, coming through the trees. Kate saw its shadow first, then her mouth fell open in astonishment as the approaching vehicle crested the rise and sped down the slope towards them.

It was a sleigh. It was wooden, whiter than the snow, with gleaming silver runners. It was led by four beautiful reindeer with shining pelts and firm, glossy antlers, and driven by a small, bearded man in a pointy hat. Reclining in the luxurious seat of the sleigh was a beautiful, raven-haired woman, with ice-white skin beneath an elaborate crown, dressed in silver furs and expensive-looking leather gloves.

At a crack of the driver's whip, the reindeer slowed to a canter and the sleigh began to swish to a halt.

The Doctor raised his eyebrows.

Kate grabbed his arm. 'Doctor, it's—'

The Doctor's voice was a soft mutter. 'Just go with the flow. Let me do the talking.'

He strode towards the sleigh, insouciant, hands in pockets. Kate hurried to keep up with him.

'And whatever you do,' said the Doctor, 'don't eat the Turkish Delight.'

'Did you hear that?' asked Reece.

'No,' said Chantelle, irritated. She ran forward through the unnaturally green undergrowth, marvelling at the feel of the artificial sun on her face.

Chantelle didn't get out into the countryside much. She thought it was a weird place – full of odd things that made snorting noises and left dung on the ground. She got nervous around horses and cows. She was a city girl – you knew where you were with people, and with shops and cars and buses and the stench of petrol.

And yet, now, looking at the beautiful forest which they'd somehow managed to construct in the middle of Hyperville, she wondered if she had been missing out on something.

'I definitely heard something,' said Reece worriedly. 'Why's there nobody else around?'

A second later there was a whooshing noise in the air, and an arrow landed in the mud at Chantelle's feet. She leapt backwards, almost knocking her brother over. Chantelle pulled the arrow out of the ground and gazed at it in wonder.

'What's that?' she murmured. 'Another message?'

'A warning,' said the voice from the undergrowth.

They gasped, and turned to face the direction the voice had come from. Nobody was to be seen.

'A warning to stay out of Sherwood Forest,' said the voice again – a woman's voice, soft and clear, coming from behind them now. Reece and Chantelle spun round again.

A woman emerged, detaching herself silently from the shadows where she had been invisible. She was beautiful, with an oval, elfin face framed by reddish-gold ringlets, and she wore a long, plain, green dress adorned with a simple wooden crucifix. But the thing they noticed most about her was that she was wielding a sturdy bow, with the arrow strung and pointing straight at them.

'Maid Marian!' said Chantelle softly.

'You are spies,' said the woman's soft voice. 'Spies for the Sheriff of Nottingham.'

'No, no,' said Chantelle hurriedly. 'Really, we're not. We just came here to explore. If it's a problem, we'll… get off, won't we, Reece?'

'Yeah. Sure,' said Reece. 'Get off. Right away.'

'You are spies,' said the woman again. 'Spies for the Sheriff of Nottingham.'

Chantelle narrowed her eyes. There was something not quite right about this Maid Marian. Her face was too chiselled and perfect, her movements and her speech stiff and mannered.

'Reece,' said Chantelle, 'can you hear… *clicking?*'

Maid Marian appeared to crane her neck by a few centimetres. And then by more. And more again. As Reece and Chantelle watched open-mouthed, her neck extended until it was a pale, stretchy column of glistening flesh at least half a metre long; and then it spun round in a full circle. When she turned to face them again, her eyes were glowing green.

'I have them, Robin,' she said. 'I have the spies.'

The teenagers turned to run.

On the other side of the clearing, a man stepped out to block their way. He was tall and muscular with flowing dark hair, was dressed in a green tunic and held a burnished wooden staff.

'The Hoodie himself,' muttered Chantelle. 'Now we're in trouble.'

Robin Hood smiled. It was not a friendly smile. His eyes looked blank and unresponsive.

Then, his hand twirled at the wrist, spinning his staff faster and faster until it became a deadly whirl. He began to move stiffly towards them.

Reece and Chantelle gasped and took a step backwards.

'They ain't real,' gasped Reece.

Chantelle shook her head. 'Robots or something. Like those things the Doctor deactivated in the Doomcastle!'

The green-eyed Marian smiled cruelly and her fingers tensed on the bow.

'Down!' yelled Chantelle, and she pulled Reece onto the mud with a thump.

Marian's arrow shot through the air where Reece's head had been a split second earlier.

It slammed into Robin Hood's chest with a thud.

Seconds later there was a flash of blue sparks, and Robin Hood staggered backwards, wreathed in blue smoke.

The Marian-bot had already flipped another arrow out of her quiver, and loaded it into the bow with lissom arms. She turned, spinning on one foot. Reece rolled to the edge of the clearing. The Marian-bot swung towards him, then back to Chantelle, who was still crouching on the mud, not daring to move.

'Come on, Chantelle!' Reece stretched his arm out. 'Come on!'

Maid Marian's face seemed to twitch in an eerie smile. Her fingers loosened on the arrow.

Chantelle screamed and buried her head in her hands.

There was a loud gunshot, and a pungent smell in the clearing.

A second later, Chantelle lifted her hands from her eyes and gawped in amazement. A black-uniformed security man, wearing headphones over his cap, was crouching at the edge of the clearing, his smoking pistol levelled. The bullet he had just fired had split Maid Marian's arrow in two.

The clearing was soon entirely surrounded with security men, all in black caps, black uniforms and headphones with radio-mikes. One of them dragged Reece to his feet, while another helped Chantelle to hers.

The Robin-bot was still inert, sparking and clicking, its hand still spinning the staff round and round, although more slowly than before.

The Marian-bot snarled, its eyes flashing a brighter green, and levelled another arrow at the security squad.

'We didn't get it, Mr Carson!' shouted the leader of the squad. 'Do you want it incapacitating?'

A bearded man in a dark suit strode into the clearing, quickly taking in the situation. 'Wait,' he snapped. 'Don't damage it.'

He twisted the dial of his watch. An almost-unbearable whining sound tore through the forest, hurting Chantelle's eardrums – she and Reece clamped their hands over their ears, realising now why the guards wore headphones.

The Marian-bot dropped its bow and bent over suddenly as if hit in the stomach, its white hands against its white temples, head rotating from side to side.

The dark-suited man made another adjustment to the dial, and the whining sound increased in pitch.

The Marian-bot's legs collapsed beneath it like those of a broken doll. A second later it keeled over and hit the artificial forest floor, its auburn nylon ringlets spread out in a fan on the mud.

Reece and Chantelle, breathing heavily, slowly got to their feet.

The man smoothed down his jacket and strode over to them, holding out his hand. 'Max Carson, Director of Operations. I'm so sorry about this. I do hope this… minor malfunction has not inconvenienced you in any way.'

Chantelle gave him a look. 'If that's what you call a minor malfunction, matey, I'd hate to see a big one.'

Max Carson smiled inscrutably. 'I do apologise. Hyperville is at the cutting edge of this kind of interactive theme-park technology. There are inevitably certain… teething troubles with some exhibits. You will of course be offered a full refund, plus gift vouchers on your Hypercards to the value of—'

'That ain't what I'd call teething troubles, mate!' Chantelle snapped. 'You got yourself a psycho Maid Marian and a bunch of Hammer Horror loonies on the loose in the Doomcastle! This place is a flamin' *deathtrap!*'

Reece thumped her elbow. 'Chantelle! The man was gonna offer us a freebie!' He looked hopefully up at Max. 'How much, mate?'

But Max Carson's diplomatic smile had already vanished, and now his face tautened. 'You were in the Doomcastle earlier? I see.' He nodded to the security squad leader. 'Take these two… children to Hospitality Suite Nine and ensure they are fed. Please don't allow them to leave under any circumstances!'

He turned, hands behind his back, and began to stride off into the forest.

'You can't do that!' Chantelle yelled. 'We've seen things! We can tell the papers!'

Max Carson stopped, looked over his shoulder. 'My dear young lady,' he said. 'You won't be telling anybody about anything. Not for a very long time.'

And then Chantelle felt her hands pinned behind her back, and, like Reece, had a gun shoved into her ribs.

'Let's go, missy,' said the security man. 'Don't give us any trouble.'

Chantelle glared at him. 'Call me *missy* again, sunshine,' she said, 'and you'll really find out what trouble means… All right, all right. We're moving…'

In the white snow and the glittering lights of the WinterZone, the Snow Queen's head slowly turned to look at the Doctor and Kate.

'Greetings, visitors,' she said softly. 'And what, pray, are you?'

The Doctor grinned. 'Ohhh, that's gooooood. I like that. Another one!'

Kate glared up at him. 'Another one?'

'Animatronic synchro-thesp. Basically a very clever, *very* advanced kind of theme-park exhibit.' He leaned down and spoke very quietly to her. 'She's not real. None of them are.'

Kate was astonished. She had done her reading-up on the refurbishments to the latest Zones in Hyperville, but nothing had quite prepared her for the wealth of detail in the Experiences, nor the level of sophistication which Sir Gerry's technical people had obviously put into their development.

'Right,' said Kate. 'So… what do we do?'

'I imagine we have a little chat,' said the Doctor. 'Right, your Maj?'

The Queen's head turned to look at Kate, then back towards the Doctor again. 'Answer me at once, or I shall lose my patience!'

'Sparking,' said the Doctor softly, and his eyes widened.

'What?' Kate looked up at him, confused.

'Sparking! *Get down!*'

The Doctor pulled Kate down into the snow, under the cover of a fallen tree-trunk.

A second later the Queen, eyes glowing red, leapt from the sleigh with astonishing agility, booted feet landing with a firm *plump* and a shower of snow. Kate, heart pounding, heard a sound. It was like a gunshot, but hollower, stranger – and a second later a bolt of crimson fire sizzled through the air and hit the tree beside them. Pink smoke billowed from the artificial trunk as it burned.

She looked at the Doctor in horror. 'Animatronic synchro-thesp, right?'

'Right.' He had put his glasses on and was peering cautiously over the tree-trunk.

'Doctor, I hate to be a pedant, but that thing is off the sledge and *moving.*'

'I had noticed.' The Doctor's answer was curt, grim, with his teeth clamped together.

'Well?'

Kate could hear the Queen's boots thudding on the fake snow. She looked up into the twinkling lights – LED lights, she assumed, high up there in a domed canopy – and hoped desperately that her life wasn't about to end in a daft, Christmassy Hell, at the hands of a demented robot.

Kate risked a glance up, over the Doctor's shoulders.

'I e animatronic Queen had her hands out in front of her. She looked as if she was feeling her way in the air.

'Interesting,' murmured the Doctor. 'Must be working on heat and motion. Visual receptors aren't properly aligned yet.'

'What are you *talking* about?' Kate hissed.

He looked at her and grinned. 'Keep still and try not to sweat. And when I say run,' he added, 'run. Head for the trees.'

'And then what? Look for a lamp post?'

Kate was being facetious, but the Doctor beamed. 'Good idea!' His hand bunched some of the snow into a ball the size of a grapefruit. 'Ready?'

Kate swallowed hard, trying to ignore the shaking and tingling sensation in her body.

For a second there was no sound but the thudding of the Queen's boots on the snow.

Then the Doctor tensed.

'Run!' he ordered, and in the same instant he threw his snowball at a nearby rock. The snowball splattered into chunks, and an instant later a sizzling bolt of red light hit the rock, smashing it into smoking shards.

Kate glimpsed it as she ran, blindly, into the trees, gasping, her breath angry and chilled, her heart thumping wildly. She screamed as she lost her footing and fell, but the Doctor was close behind her and grabbed her arm, helping her up.

'Keep looking,' he said grimly. 'We've got to find a way to get out of here.' As he spoke, he was looking around, and picked up a flat, broad chunk of icy rock from the ground.

'What are you going to do with that?' Kate asked.

'Something clever, I hope.' He grabbed her arm again. 'Keep running!'

'But what *is* it?' Kate gasped as they hurtled through the trees. 'Has it got a gun, or something?'

'I've got a nasty suspicion,' the Doctor said, glancing over his shoulder. He pulled a small compass-like object out of his

pocket. 'Come on, come on. Need some energy readings...
Ahhh! *Molto bene!* There! Come on!'

Zigzagging through the trees, the Doctor ran, seemingly
taking a random path. And there, suddenly, to Kate's
astonishment, was something else in the snow in front of
them – as tall as a tree, but not a tree. Black, metallic, gleaming.
An old-fashioned Victorian lamp post.

'What did I tell you?' The Doctor gave Kate a triumphant
grin.

'Doctor!' Kate glanced nervously over her shoulder.

For a second, she and the Doctor turned together to look.

The Queen was *running* through the forest.

Kate saw her blank, white face, her cloak streaming out
behind her and her arms and legs moving with the firm,
steady rhythm of a distance runner. She was heading straight
for them.

And there was something wrong with her *hand*—

'OK. Go forward. Quickly!'

Kate stepped in the direction where the Doctor was
pointing, into the cover of some denser undergrowth.

She moved forwards, realising that the chill was abating
and the undergrowth around her was masking a tunnel, a
man-made shaft with smooth sides. She stepped forwards and
found herself up against a soft, plastic divider. She pushed—

—and, after staggering through a short tunnel, she emerged
blinking into the lights of Hyperville.

She was in the Grand Atrium of the FunGlobe, with the
huge, segmented glass dome stretching over her head and the
great, sweeping stairs of the Central Exhibition dominating
the marble-floored space. People milled around, eating,

drinking and buying postcards, voices echoing upwards into the cathedral-like space, oblivious to her.

Kate looked backwards. 'Doctor!' she called. Then, more loudly, '*Doctor!*'

The Doctor burst out of the tunnel, backwards. 'Get everyone out of the area,' he told her.

'What?' Kate looked confused.

'Clear the area! Now!'

People at the nearby restaurant tables and shop entrances were looking curiously at Kate and the Doctor, muttering.

For a moment, Kate was flustered – but only for a moment. She could see two security men on the stairs, clocked one of them answering something on his headpiece and saw them racing down towards her and the Doctor.

High above them, a swooping Oculator saw everything.

In his office, Sir Gerry was drinking champagne with Paul Kendrick and Shaneeqi, looking out from the picture window onto the thronged malls below.

Miss Devonshire, immaculate as ever in her red jacket and skirt and her rimless glasses, stood slightly apart with her hands neatly folded.

'Impressive place, Sir Gerry,' said Paul, nodding.

Sir Gerry beamed. 'I'm glad you think so, lad. Grown extensively over the last few years, of course. A lot of it's thanks to Max and Miss Devonshire and some spot-on development at Carson Polymers.'

'I know about them,' said Paul. 'We got shares in them, I think.' He had tucked his mirror-shades into his breast-pocket, revealing intense, sea-blue eyes with a penetrating stare.

'I wanna see the Zone,' said Shaneeqi, like an eager child.

She looked up at Sir Gerry, opening her big brown eyes wide. 'Can I see the Zone?'

'Yes, of course, I—'

Sir Gerry was distracted by a winking light on the panel on his vast desk. He glowered at Miss Devonshire, nodded. Miss Devonshire stabbed at a button.

'Yes?' she said, then, hearing the reply in her earpiece, 'Yes, I'll tell him. Mr Carson for you, Sir Gerry.'

Sir Gerry looked over in irritation as Max Carson's face appeared on the hidden screen on the oak-panelling. 'Max, what the 'eck's going on? I told you I didn't want disturbing!'

'Everything is under control,' said Max smoothly. 'Small security matter.'

Sir Gerry frowned. 'You sure?'

'Absolutely, sir. Everything is in hand.'

Sir Gerry puffed out his cheeks and made a small gesture of apology towards Paul Kendrick and Shaneeqi.

Unseen by Sir Gerry, Miss Devonshire gave a cold, crisp smile.

Kate ran to the nearest information-point and flipped her Access All Areas pass in front of the electronic eye on top of the cylinder. 'Kate Maguire. Get me the public address. Now!'

There was a brief whirring sound, and a click. Then a soft voice said, 'Address System enabled.'

Kate leaned into the information-point and spoke, hearing her own voice reverberating around the Atrium, amplified a thousandfold. 'Ladies and gentlemen, we would like to ask you to clear the area immediately, please. Clear the area quickly and quietly. We have, ah, we have a gas leak in the building. Please evacuate the area by the nearest exit. Thank you.'

Grumbling, looking at each other and shrugging as if they didn't quite believe it, people were grabbing bags, making their way to the exits.

'OK?' Kate shouted to the Doctor.

He was backing away from the snowy-white entrance to the WinterZone, holding on to the shiny wedge of ice-rock he had procured.

'Five seconds,' he said. 'It'll be out. I didn't have time to secure the door.'

The security men were there beside them. 'Back away, miss,' said one of them, and levelled his sub-machine gun at the Doctor's head. 'Sir, put your hands above your head and get down on the floor!'

'Don't be stupid!' snapped the Doctor. 'Get back! All of you get back!'

'Sir, I'm warning you—'

There was a crashing sound from the entrance to the WinterZone. Then the doors to the tunnel flew open, and a second later the Snow Queen, eyes blazing red, stalked from the cavernous opening...

FIVE

Kate saw the security man's eyes widen and his jaw drop open.

'I said get *back*!' the Doctor ordered. 'You as well, Kate!'

People were screaming, now, and running for the exits. Tables were upturned, postcard racks scattered, crockery smashed in the stampede.

The Snow Queen raised her arm. She pointed at the Doctor, as if accusing him of something.

As Kate watched, she saw the Snow Queen's ice-white fingers drop away where they joined the hand.

In the same moment, the hollow nozzle inside the Queen's hand seemed to explode with pink smoke. A dazzling slice of red light cut across the Atrium towards the Doctor.

Like a fencer parrying the blow, the Doctor put his hand up, catching the beam with the plastic ice and reflecting it straight back at the Snow Queen.

The beam slammed into her face, blowing the head and crown to smithereens, scattering twisted fragments across the nearby café area. The security men dropped to their knees and, somewhat belatedly, fired concentrated bursts of bullets into the Snow Queen's stomach. The Doctor winced, dropping the charred plastic.

The headless Queen, smoke pouring from her shattered neck, tottered on her booted feet and pitched slowly forward onto the marbled floor.

There was silence.

The Doctor let out a breath and picked up the burnt remains of the wedge of plastic, pulling a surprised, rueful face. 'I wondered if that would work,' he said quietly, dusting down his jacket.

Coughing and choking in the pungent smoke, her heart thumping, Kate ran forward. 'Doctor, are you all right?'

'Never better!' The Doctor gave her a reassuring grin. 'Well, I say never better. I mean, fine. Well, I *say* fine—'

'You mean tolerable, yes.' Kate was already getting used to cutting to the chase with the Doctor. 'Please, Doctor, what *was* that thing?'

The Doctor didn't look at her. His face and voice grim, he said, 'I'll tell you later. Come on.'

He and Kate turned together, and found the two security men levelling their guns at them.

'Doctor,' said Kate nervously, 'I think these guys have other ideas.' She suddenly spotted a woman with high cheekbones and short grey hair, dressed in the black security uniform and cap, striding across the Atrium. She had a pistol rather than a sub-machine gun, and walked, Kate thought, with an air of authority. 'And her,' she added nervously.

'Right!' exclaimed the Doctor. 'You in charge here?' He offered his hand to the woman, with a big smile.

'Captain Tess Tilbrook,' said the woman. 'Head of Security.' She didn't return the handshake. 'Perhaps you'd like to come with me, Doctor? Sir Gerry would like a little chat.'

'What about me?' asked Kate nervously.

Tess Tilbrook nodded. 'You as well, Miss Maguire.'

'Oh, no, no, don't involve her,' said the Doctor hastily. 'I mean, she's a Trainee. Aren't you? Things to do, places to go. I expect she's giving a hundred per cent.'

'A hundred and ten,' said Kate, with a quick smile.

'A hundred and ten. There you go.' The Doctor's smile vanished as he did a double take. 'A hundred and *ten*? You can't give a hundred and ten per cent, Kate. *Per cent*. It means out of a hundred. You can't give a hundred and ten out of a hundred.' He tilted his head. 'Although, if you were a Magnesian Centipod... Ten extra tentacles,' he said aside to Kate. 'Only for use in the summer. They do a lot of charity work, the Magnesian Centipods. Good people.'

If Tess Tilbrook was bothered by the Doctor's prattling, she didn't show it. She motioned towards the glass lift. 'This way, please. Both of you. Sir Gerry wants to see you.'

They entered the lift – Tess, then the Doctor and Kate, then the two guards. The glass doors began to close.

'Ground Floor,' said the Doctor cheerfully. 'Wigs and Haberdashery, Kitchenware and Foods. Going up!'

Kate shot him a wary look. She was beginning to wonder if she had made the right decision in associating with this strange man. But he seemed to understand the terrifying experience they had just had – and for that reason alone, it was worth sticking with him.

As the lift ascended, Kate had a grandstand view of more security guards arriving to carry away the smoking, shattered remains of the Snow Queen.

'I won't be long, Derek,' chirped Tricia Stanford, as the lift doors opened up into the penthouse apartment they were renting for the week. She descended the steps, handbag on her arm, followed by Derek, who was carrying half a dozen bulging bags.

Derek grunted, holding up the bags to ask where to put them.

'Just dump them on the sofa, love,' Tricia commanded, indicating the vast sweep of white leather couch which dominated the living space. 'And make me a cuppa, there's a dear. I'm going to have a shower. Takes it out of you, all this shopping!'

You're telling me, thought Derek miserably. He threw the bags on the sofa as Tricia disappeared into the bathroom. Then he put the kettle on and, yawning, swung his legs onto the other white sofa. He picked up the TV remote and flicked it on. The three-metre-wide plasma screen leapt into life, showing *Deal or No Deal*.

Derek hadn't been at all sure about taking a holiday in Hyperville – he didn't like the idea of the place at all. Tricia had steamrollered all his protests, as usual, and emotionally blackmailed him by pointing out all the things there were for the kids to do. Derek had fallen for it, and was now wishing he'd left them to it and gone on that golfing weekend instead.

He flicked through all the channels, tutting. From down the corridor came the sounds of splashing and singing. He shook his head, smiling ruefully. Tricia would be some time

– she always was. She was a woman who saw a shower as an experience, rather than a mere necessity.

The doorbell buzzed.

Derek groaned, hauled himself off the sofa and staggered to the door. His finger hovered over the intercom button and he hesitated. How was he going to do this?

He pressed the button and tried the hoarsest of painful whispers. 'Hello?'

'Room service,' said a crisp, slightly squeaky voice.

Odd, thought Derek. He hadn't ordered anything. Although he wouldn't have put it past Tricia to have got something in for a little post-shower snack. He sighed, and pressed the release control.

The door slid silently open.

The first thing Derek saw was the tray, holding a bottle of champagne and two glasses. It was held aloft, almost at the height of his eye-line.

Then he looked down, and saw who was holding it.

His mouth opened in a silent scream.

The metre-high dummy stalked in, its feet making a soft, squelching sound on the laminate floor. Once it was inside, it hurled the champagne tray away – tray, bottles and glass landed on a nearby armchair.

Derek backed away, his eyes bulging in horror and disbelief.

It was the same one. The midget dummy he'd seen in the shop, with its sinister red eyes, glossy black face and sculpted blonde hair – only this time dressed like a miniature waitress, in a little white button-tunic and black trousers. Its head swivelled from side to side and he was sure he could hear it quietly *chuckling*.

'Room service,' said the voice again. It sounded to Derek like some demented doll's voice, recorded on tape – the sort of thing you'd pull a cord to hear. '*Room service. Room service.*'

Derek grabbed the nearest thing available, which was the TV remote, and pointed it at the dummy like a weapon. He tried to croak a threat, but this time his throat just wouldn't let him.

The dummy cackled, and launched itself into the air with a back-flip.

Derek ducked, and the dummy whooshed over his head.

He heard a squelching sound and looked up to see that it had attached itself to the ceiling, its small plastic hands and feet softening and moulding themselves into sucker-shapes so that it could cling on.

Derek backed away so quickly that he fell into the coffee table and knocked it over. Magazines and cups went flying.

The dummy's eyes glowed red and the unearthly chuckle echoed through the room again.

Derek found himself sprawled on the floor with the dummy clinging to the ceiling above him, its head twisting round to look at him and those malevolent red eyes drilling into him.

And then it sprang.

'The thing I want to know is,' said the Doctor, 'why *coffee?*'

'I beg your pardon?' Sir Gerry raised his eyebrows.

'Coffee!' said the Doctor. 'In the shops, everywhere. Why do these places always smell of it? Just strikes me as odd, that's all. Some people might not actually *like* coffee.' He leaned back in the guest chair in Sir Gerry's office and was about to put his feet up on the desk before he thought better of it.

At the picture window, Sir Gerry turned round and narrowed his eyes at Kate. 'Miss Maguire,' he said, 'I gather this feller has summat to do with you?'

'He can help you, Sir Gerry,' said Kate, leaning forward. 'The Doctor's picked up on all sorts of things going wrong in Hyperville. It's not just the Snow Queen. Tell him, Doctor.'

Sir Gerry leaned on his desk, breathing heavily, and turned his gaze towards the Doctor. 'I'll have you know, Doctor, that my Director of Operations, Max Carson, was all for having you thrown out on your ear.'

'Ah, yes.' The Doctor scratched his ear awkwardly. 'Black suit, tries to be terribly butch? Little George Michael-y thing going on with the beard? Yes, we've met.'

'But I,' Sir Gerry went on, 'have been in this damn business long enough to know when I see an opportunity. And you, Doctor, are an opportunity.' He sank back into his chair, nodding and smiling. 'That's why I asked my security officer to bring you directly to me, rather than to Max.' Sir Gerry nodded towards Captain Tilbrook, who was standing impassively at the door to the office. 'You know you've been giving Maxie-boy quite a runaround?'

'Have I? Oh. Sorry.'

'I'm sure you are, Doctor. Go on, then. Amaze me. Tell me what you want me to know.'

The Doctor leaned forward, his face suddenly serious and urgent. 'Sir Gerry, you have a serious problem. You have dangerous automata in some of your Zones. Close down the Doomcastle and WinterZone. Don't let *anybody* into them, not until I've had a chance to have a proper look at them.'

'Until *you've* had a chance?' Sir Gerry chortled and raised an eyebrow. 'What exactly are *your* qualifications for doing that?'

The Doctor opened his mouth, closed it again, pulled a face. 'Weeell… To be honest, I'm pretty much good at everything.'

'Everything?' Sir Gerry's bushy eyebrows shot up.

'OK, some of the Entertainment questions on Trivial Pursuit throw me a bit. I forget which era I'm supposed to be playing in. Really hard to get a pink wedge on the— Sorry, sorry. You were saying?'

Sir Gerry sighed and leaned forward, hands clasped on the desk. 'You see, Doctor, I do have a bit of a dilemma. I've got a business to run, and sometimes mavericks can be helpful. Now, then, if you've genuinely got summat to offer me, how about you clear off out there and find some evidence?'

'He is right, sir,' said Tess Tilbrook. 'We did have a seriously malfunctioning WinterZone exhibit.' She stepped forward, exchanging glances with the Doctor. 'We got everyone out of the Atrium in time, but it could have caused serious damage.'

The Doctor leapt to his feet, pushing his hair back with both hands. 'Ohhhh, humans, humans, *huuuu-mans*! It's more than a seriously malfunctioning exhibit!' He leaned with both hands on Sir Gerry's desk, his voice low and urgent. 'That… *thing*, Sir Gerry, Captain Tilbrook, that thing which your guards only managed to disable once I'd reflected its own weapon back on it… Do you want to know what it was? It was an Auton. Ever heard of that? An *Auton*.'

Sir Gerry sat back in his chair. 'An… Auton? What the bloomin' Nora is that?'

The Doctor's voice was low and urgent. 'A fragment of the Nestene Consciousness. An alien race able to manifest itself in a range of forms, with a biological make-up congruent with the molecular structure of Earth plastics. They've tried to invade this planet at least three times before and almost succeeded. Now, I think this could be one left over from a previous invasion attempt. And the way you're looking at me, I might as well be speaking Swahili.' The Doctor turned his head and looked at Kate. 'I'm not, am I? Speaking Swahili?'

'No,' she said reassuringly.

'Good. Just checking. You see, you probably don't *remember* any of it. People never do, that's the problem.' The Doctor leaned on Sir Gerry's desk and opened his eyes wide. 'And do you know what? I think the malfunctioning exhibits in the Doomcastle may have been Nestene constructs as well.'

'Really,' said Sir Gerry levelly.

'Maybe not full Autons. Not total capability. But ohhh, yes, they looked alien to me, Sir Gerry. Now, I *need* to know if these were just odd remnants left behind from a previous invasion, or if they're trying to establish a new bridgehead. People could be in danger, Sir Gerry.'

Sir Gerry shook his head and snorted. 'Poppycock! Doctor, I've listened to your twaddle for long enough. So, thank you for the customer feedback – it's been noted. You're free to go.' He gestured towards the door.

'Oh. And that's *all*? You're not going to close down any of the Zones? Evacuate any of the people, seal any areas off?' The Doctor sounded incredulous.

Sir Gerry smiled. 'As Miss Maguire will no doubt tell you, I am running a business here, lad. A major, thriving, 24-hour-a-day *business*.' He glanced at his watch. 'Hyperville's gearing up for night-shift, and the bars and casinos are about to open. You got any idea how much money I'd lose if I closed the place? Just for one night? The damage would be irreparable.'

'Just give me *two hours*. Suspend trading, get everyone

out, and let me check over all the Zones for you, deactivate anything potentially dangerous.'

'Sorry, Doctor. No can do.' Sir Gerry lit a cigar.

'Ohhhhh... .' The Doctor gritted his teeth. 'Please don't say *no can do*. I really hate that. Do you talk about *blue-skies thinking* as well?'

Sir Gerry sighed. 'One more thing, Doctor. Before you toddle off.' He waggled his cigar in the Doctor's direction.

'Yes?'

'Mr Carson detected you messing about with a... sonic pen of some sort. You did summat odd with the Hypercard vending network?'

'Really?' The Doctor tried to look innocent. 'No idea.'

Sir Gerry held out his hand. 'Hand it over, Doctor. You'll get it back when you leave Hyperville. Gaffer's word.'

The Doctor's face fell, and he looked like a naughty schoolboy as he handed the thick, pen-like silver instrument to Sir Gerry. 'Take care of it,' he said. 'I don't want it broken.'

Sir Gerry smiled, and slipped the device into his desk drawer. 'Taken care of, Doctor.' He slammed the drawer shut. 'Now, then, happen you'd like to do a little shopping? I think you'll find we're open all night...'

The doors to the Great Hall of the Doomcastle flew open with a crash.

Two armed guards stormed into the Hall, leaping onto the table and covering all exits with their guns.

Max Carson strode in after them, looking cool and calm, hands behind his back, his dark eyes flicking back and forth. He was flanked by six more security guards.

'Search,' he ordered them.

Max Carson enjoyed power.

Four years ago, he had been a nobody. He'd had a job title – Managing Director of Carson Polymers, for what that was worth. They were a small firm with a small turnover, and his empire had consisted of one prefab office and one small factory warehouse, which he staffed with cheap labour from Eastern Europe. They'd had their regular customers – a selection of local firms whose orders were starting to tail off as the global downturn bit hard. And Max knew it was only going to get worse. One day, he went into the office, put his briefcase down on his desk as usual and decided that the time had come to call in the administrators.

He had one appointment later that day, a meeting with a Miss Elizabeth Devonshire about a possible new project. But he knew that one new order, even if it came off, wouldn't be big enough to keep Carson Polymers afloat.

However, his meeting with Miss Devonshire was the one which changed Max Carson's life.

Thinking back, he couldn't really remember much about it. There had been talk of wonderful new opportunities, of riding out the global recession to a new consumer boom. Of an age of plastic. Of spend, spend, spend. And Max had gradually realised that he was being asked to be part of this. Miss Devonshire, it transpired, worked as a head-hunter and general aide to Sir Gerry Hobbes-Mayhew, the self-made magnate, the man who had a global empire of shopping and leisure centres and who had recently poured all of his investments into one place – *Hyperville*.

Max knew all about Hyperville. It was always on the news. Opening soon. Bold new statement, they said. Revolutionising leisure and shopping for the entire population, they said. He didn't quite believe it until he saw the place himself. And then, that same day, he was offered the position of Director of Operations.

Max knew it was a once-in-a-lifetime chance. He didn't stop to ask himself what lay behind the strange offer. He just grabbed it with both hands.

It all became clear, of course, later on. Who Miss Devonshire really was. Who she was working for. And it was clear, too, why Carson Polymers was still needed – because Miss Devonshire's employers were people for whom plastic had a very, very special significance.

Carson Polymers was kept on, as a subsidiary of Hyperville Holdings. It had new investment, new staff – properly trained technicians, this time, not the minimum-wage labour he'd used before. It was used to develop something amazing – something Max knew could revolutionise the way people lived. Something called Plastinol.

And here, now, he didn't always stop to think how far he had come in the past few years. Sometimes it was all like a dream – and Max Carson feared that he might one day wake up.

Max snapped his fingers and pointed to the fallen figures of the witches. 'Check there are no more of *those*,' he said quietly, as he strode down the hall to take a look at the figure of Dracula, who was standing slumped like a broken puppet.

Carefully, Max pushed the vampire-automaton's head back, peering into its eyes, before slapping a red disc on its plastic hand. The disc glowed slightly in the dark, and the automaton's knees buckled, causing it to fall to the ground with a crash. He then fixed similar discs on the inert figures of the witches.

Max gave a grim smile of satisfaction, and tapped the Bluetooth attachment in his ear.

'The rogue units are deactivated,' he said. 'I think we have bought ourselves a little time again.'

Miss Devonshire's voice came back to him. 'I hate to tell you this, Max,' she said, 'but there's still one unaccounted for.'

'Which one?' he asked quietly.

'Beta-4. From the ShopZone.'

'Ahh!' Max gave a rueful grin. 'The little one.'

'As you say. The little one. Track it down and neutralise it, Max. We don't want it doing any serious damage, not yet. Not until the Central Program comes online.'

Max nodded. 'I'll do that.'

'Good boy, Max. I'll have a biscuit waiting.'

He clicked the link off, and sighed. 'This,' he said to nobody in particular, 'is turning into one of those days.'

SIX

'**S**hopping,' said the Doctor, as they descended in the glittering travelator. He was watching the crowds bustling to and fro in the malls and walkways, Kate noticed, and all the while checking readings on the compass-like instrument he had been using in the WinterZone. 'Shopping, shopping… It's an *odd* thing, isn't it? I mean, as a hobby.'

Kate shrugged. She didn't think so. 'What do you mean?'

'You spend time trying on different variations of the same shirt or the same coat, make a whole afternoon of it, even, bring your friends… And then you take your card or your cash to the counter, after you've chosen the one that's most like what you had in mind. But it's never quite the way you imagined it would be.'

'That's the thing,' she explained patiently. 'The stuff looks good in the shop because it's with all the other stuff.'

The Doctor clicked his tongue. 'I went shopping in New

York with Shirley Bassey once. Never again. *Blimey*, that woman can try on shoes…'

'Bit of a Big Spender, was she?'

'Oh, very good. You see, we're getting on so well.'

Kate smiled. 'Don't name-drop, Doctor. It doesn't impress me… Anyway, I think this is a wonderful place.'

'And also a strange place.' The Doctor nodded upwards at the Oculator as it bounced overhead. 'Why do you reckon that's there?'

'It keeps us safe,' Kate said with a shrug.

'Safe?' The Doctor wrinkled his nose and looked down at her. 'How does an electronic box of tricks watching your every move keep you *safe*? Safe from what?'

Kate folded her arms and glared at him. 'The world's changed, Doctor. People are happy to give up a little privacy these days, for the sake of being more secure.'

The Doctor pulled a face. 'Hmm. "They who can give up essential liberty to obtain a little temporary safety, deserve neither liberty nor safety." Ever heard that?' He looked at Kate. 'Benjamin Franklin,' he added.

'Oh, yes. Inventor of the lightning conductor.'

'And bifocals. Don't forget bifocals. Demon chess player, too. Almost beat me a few times.' The Doctor was still staring at the device he held. 'You know, I'm getting some really *odd* readings on this.'

'What's that?' Kate said.

'It's a liminal sub-wave energy detector. Tells me if there's anything here that shouldn't be.'

'And is there?' she asked, interested.

'I'm not sure,' admitted the Doctor. 'Readings are fluctuating…'

'Sir Gerry didn't seem to want to give you the time of day,' she said, amused.

The Doctor sighed. 'Thing is, Kate, the universe is full of Sir Gerrys. Self-made millionaire, plain-talking, essentially a decent man but can't see further than his own nose. Very frustrating people to deal with… And he's not twigged about you, has he? Don't you find that odd?'

She shrugged. 'I'm very convincing.'

'You're not very modest. Tell me something else. The Hypercards. Show me.'

Kate handed him her Hypercard. 'You can access the network with a card, do direct debits. It's great.'

'Mmm. I'm sure.' The Doctor, who didn't sound convinced, handed Kate her card back.

Kate sighed. 'You know what? I think you're one of those guys who doesn't like competent women.'

The Doctor looked hurt. 'What makes you think that?'

She knew she had upset him, but carried on. 'I bet you just like to be *admired*, don't you? Show off with your clever boxes of tricks and gizmos? And have someone hanging on your elbow going all slack-jawed and saying it's all *brilliant*? Well, I'm not like that. I'm not easily impressed.'

The Doctor grinned. 'Good! Neither am I.'

As they disembarked, the Doctor nodded at the huge, cliff-like façade of Total Records, stretching up ten floors above them, its cavernous entrance thumping with techno. 'Although that… that *is* impressive. That singer you were telling me about,' he said thoughtfully. 'That her?'

Kate looked up at the twenty-metre-high rendition of Shaneeqi's sharp, pretty features and spiked scarlet hair, a colourful Warhol-style print emblazoned in shimmering plastic across the glass frontage of the store. She smiled, nodded. 'That's her. The lovely Shaneeqi. I had the pleasure earlier today.'

'And this… Zone of hers that's being launched. In the casino, you said? You got an invitation?'

Kate flipped her badge up at him. 'Access All Areas, Doc. Does what it says on the tin.'

'Oh, no, no, don't do the Doc thing. Anyway, look, I need to be there. See if I can mingle with the crowd. Be alert. Find out what's going on here.'

'You really think there could be danger here?' Kate asked.

'Oh, yes.' The Doctor gave her a casual, sideways glance, hands in pockets, and swivelled towards her with a slight smile when she didn't look too perturbed. 'You OK with that?' he asked, mouth half-open and eyebrows raised.

'I'm fine with that.'

'Good! I'm starting to like you, Kate Maguire.'

Kate smiled. Again, she felt the hard, comforting oblong of the Hypercard in her inside pocket and wondered if now was the time. Somehow she knew it was not. She folded her arms. 'You *could* evacuate this entire place in a matter of minutes, you know. Hit a fire alarm.'

The Doctor pulled an awkward face. 'That could cause more problems than it solves. And anyway – we could be talking just a couple of rogue Autons, randomly activated after years. I've seen that kind of thing happen before.' He seemed to stare into space as he spoke to her, but his tone was low and urgent. 'No point causing a mass panic. Last thing we want to do. You know what humans are like.'

Kate gave him a curious look. 'Yes, Doctor. We are human.'

'Speak for yourself.'

'What do you—'

'Now that's odd,' said the Doctor, who had suddenly put his glasses on and was staring across the mall at one of the upper balcony levels.

'What?'

'Up there. Some heavies in a bit of a hurry!' The Doctor pointed, and now Kate saw – about half a dozen black-uniformed security officers were hurrying through the shoppers, guns unholstered, pounding along the artificial pavements towards one of the lifts. 'Come on!' The Doctor leapt onto the nearest escalator and ran upwards, with Kate hurrying behind.

Max Carson was enjoying a tea break.

'English tea, Miss Devonshire,' he said, sipping from the bone china cup. 'One of life's few genuine little pleasures.' His voice echoed around the vast, echoing chamber on Level Zero.

Miss Devonshire sat, legs crossed, in her leather swivel-chair, which appeared to be the only item of furniture in the vast space. She was, as usual, immaculate in her skirt, jacket, crisp white blouse and shiny, calf-length boots. Her rimless glasses shone under the dim, greenish lighting.

'Plastinol-2,' said Miss Devonshire. 'It worked on the journalist woman, Andrea. It worked *exactly* as it was meant to. Reading the structure of her DNA and replicating itself. Given a boost of energy, there's no reason why Plastinol-2 couldn't do so on a wider scale.' Miss Devonshire smiled, and peered at him over her glasses. 'Tell me about the test activations?'

He smiled apologetically. 'Things got… a little livelier than we'd anticipated. As you know, we had some rogue units. Beta-4 is still on the loose, but my people are on it.'

Miss Devonshire pressed her elegant, red-nailed fingers together. 'And Max – when *can* we expect the Central Program to be ready?'

'There's still a good forty-eight hours' work to be done for it to run in a stable fashion. Then it needs to be tested—'

Miss Devonshire held her hand up. 'What if it were to run within *twelve* hours, Max?'

Max Carson stopped pacing, put his cup down on his saucer and stared at her. 'That would have… interesting workload repercussions,' he admitted.

'But it could be done?'

'Yes – in theory – but the testing…'

Miss Devonshire got to her feet and strolled over to face Max, eye-to-eye. She raised her elegant eyebrows. 'It will be tested when it runs, Max. I grow weary.'

She turned, and looked for the first time at the source of the soft green light in the hangar.

'I grow weary,' she repeated, 'and so does the Consciousness.'

One vast wall of the chamber bulged inwards, the convex bump translucent and phosphorescent. As Max and Miss Devonshire watched, it pulsed and a low, shuddering sound – very like a growl – echoed through the space, the sound shaking the walls and reverberating in Max's eardrums.

Miss Devonshire rounded angrily on him. 'Twelve hours, Max. The Central Program comes online before dawn.'

'That'll be difficult,' Max insisted again.

Miss Devonshire pursed her lips. 'But not impossible.'

Max nodded reluctantly.

A wide, red smile flashed across Miss Devonshire's face, and vanished almost in the same instant. 'Good. Then the moment is almost at hand.'

She strode to the wall, reaching out her hands, softly caressing the pulsating bump as if it were the face of a child. The green light filled the lenses of her glasses.

'Tonight's little diversion is all ready?'

Max nodded. 'All the pieces are in place.'

'That will be the final trial. And then,' Miss Devonshire whispered, 'the time of flesh on this paltry planet will be at an end, and a new era will be upon us… The age of plastic. The Nestenes in all their forms will rise up, gain strength, eradicate all pathetic attempts to oppose their dominance. And from here – from this world so rich in oils and nutrients and gels and plastics – they will establish a base from which to rise up and *conquer.*'

She broke away, lowering her hands, and snapped her head round to face Max.

'But first,' she added with a smile, 'do finish your tea.'

Max smiled nervously, and sipped.

Kate and the Doctor had followed the guards through the luxurious foyer of the Hyperville Hotel, and up to Floor Seven, just in time to see the armed squad clattering down the corridor towards one particular door.

Kate was about to follow them, but the Doctor pulled her back, making her wait for a few seconds behind a laundry trolley. Only when he was ready did he saunter out into the corridor, hands in pockets, looking as if he owned the place.

The door to room 776 was open. Kate could see a plush, blue-carpeted lounge, where a woman in a bathrobe was sobbing on a big, curved white leather couch. Nervously, Kate stepped inside. One of the security men noticed her and held her back.

'I don't think you'd better, miss.'

Kate flipped her badge up so the man could read it. 'Access All Areas, it says. From Sir Gerry himself.'

'Yes, miss,' said the security man awkwardly, 'but I don't think he means you to see this.'

The Doctor, however, was already inside, peering over the guards' shoulders at the prone form on the floor.

'It's Derek!' he said in astonishment.

Six snub-nosed machine guns were thrust under the Doctor's chin. He backed off, holding up his hands. 'All right, all right. No need to get like that. I know this man. Please let me see him.'

Tricia broke off from her sobbing and looked up, peering through her hands at the Doctor. 'It's you,' she said, uncertainly. 'Do you know what happened to Derek?'

The Doctor gulped. 'Well, if these gentlemen could let me have a look, I might be able to say.' He raised his eyebrows hopefully. 'I am a doctor,' he added. 'The Doctor. Sir Gerry knows me. Check with Captain Tilbrook.'

The leader of the squad glowered at the Doctor for a second and then muttered into the radio-link on his collar. The Doctor gave Kate an encouraging look, and she smiled nervously.

'Well?' the Doctor asked.

The man nodded, and the Doctor leaned down beside the inert body of Derek, peering at him with a magnifying glass.

Kate peered over his shoulder, not wanting to look too closely. She'd not seen a dead body before – not a human one, anyway. She remembered when her dog had died when she was 10, and that had been traumatic enough.

'I'm sorry. I'm so sorry.' The Doctor straightened up, looking uncomfortably over at Tricia.

On the other side of the room, Tricia had her face in her hands. 'We was going to do so much,' she wailed. 'Had a cruise booked for next year. And painting the living room.' Her hand went up to her mouth and she shook, tears streaming down her face. 'We had such a job deciding between Ocean Breeze and Coral Beauty. Now he'll never get to see it. Oh, Derek.'

She was led out by two of the guards.

The Doctor looked up at the ceiling directly above Derek's inert form. 'Now, I wonder how *that* got there?'

'What?' Kate asked.

The Doctor nodded to the burliest security man. 'Give me a hand, would you? Lift up?'

The man looked at his superior, who gave him a grudging nod. He got down on one knee, forming a firm lattice with his thick fingers, and the Doctor, nodding gratefully, stepped onto it with one foot.

'Much obliged!' said the Doctor. 'And lift!'

With the burly security guard supporting his foot, the Doctor peered at the marks he had found on the ceiling of the lounge. He pulled a specimen jar and a spatula from his capacious pockets and scraped at the surface, scratching off some of whatever he had found into the jar.

'All right, big feller! Back down we go!'

The Doctor hopped back down to ground level and slipped the specimen jar into his pocket.

'Right then, everyone!,' he said. 'This man's been murdered. Strangled. I suggest you seal off the area. You're looking for an assailant with an incredibly powerful grip, the ability to move extremely fast, and also to hang upside-down from the ceiling. Oh, and wearing size 12 shoes. That's a child's size 12, by the way.'

'A child?' said a familiar voice from the doorway. Captain Tess Tilbrook strode in and faced the Doctor. 'Doctor, you're not seriously suggesting the assailant was a *child*?'

'No, Captain Tilbrook,' said the Doctor quietly. 'Something worse.'

She frowned. 'What, then? A dwarf?'

'Something like that.' The Doctor's expression, Kate noticed, had turned from flippant to hard and cold within the space of a second. 'A homicidal homunculus.'

Tess stared at the Doctor for a moment. Kate knew she was sizing up whether he was mad, or deadly serious.

'I'll get Sir Gerry to evacuate Hyperville,' she said.

'No, no, no.' The Doctor shook his head firmly. 'That will only cause panic, and panic can get people killed. Especially if the Nestenes realise we're on to them and start moving earlier than planned... What kind of weapons have your people got?'

Tess looked at him curiously. 'Why do you ask?'

'I'm just asking myself if they're going to be enough. That's all.' The Doctor looked upwards again. 'I wonder where it went?... Aha!' He leapt up onto the back of the couch and tapped on a black grille high in the wall. 'Ventilation duct! Well, I'm not getting in there. But I bet that's where it went.' To Kate's astonishment, he pulled his sonic device out and shone it inside, using its blue light like a torch.

'I thought you gave that to Sir Gerry?' she said.

'What I gave to Sir Gerry,' said the Doctor, peering intently into the ventilation duct, 'was a portable immersion heater.' He shot her a quick grin. 'Very good for warming up coffee in thirty seconds.'

Kate folded her arms and shook her head in wonderment. 'He'll find out! So where did you get that from? Planet Zog?'

'No. Argos,' the Doctor said, his voice still thoughtful, as he hopped back down to floor level.

Tess Tilbrook had been looking from one of them to the other, trying to speak. 'Doctor, you said *it* just now. As if the murderer isn't human.'

'Oh, it isn't,' said the Doctor cheerfully. 'Not remotely human.' He gave Tess a hard, serious look. 'Hunt it down. Find it. Before it finds anybody else.'

'And what are you going to do?'

'I need to find out properly what else is going on here. Look, is there… is there anywhere in Hyperville that the public are prevented from going?'

Tess Tilbrook shrugged. 'Sure. Hundreds of service tunnels, maintenance areas, storage floors… Where do you start?'

'Anywhere *you* can't go? Anywhere just Max Carson or Miss Devonshire can access, for example?'

'Not that I know of. But this place is the size of a small city.'

The Doctor nodded. 'All right. Keep Sir Gerry informed. Not Mr Carson – I don't trust him. Be careful. The Nestenes can pull all sorts of tricks. They can even make plastic facsimiles of human beings. Come on, Kate… Kate?'

Her phone was beeping, and she was checking texts. 'I need to meet up with Sir Gerry,' she said. 'We've all got a rendezvous in two hours.'

'Better be there, then,' said the Doctor. 'I've got a few errands to take care of.'

'How do I know I can trust *you*, Doctor?' Tess Tilbrook called after him.

He stopped in the doorway. 'I deactivated the Snow Queen, didn't I? Without that, two of your men would be dead. At least... Look, do something for me. Help Mrs Stanford find her children.'

'Children?'

'She has two teenage children. Reece and Chantelle. Get them all put into another suite.'

'Anything else?' Tess asked sarcastically.

'Actually, yes.' The Doctor turned on one heel and, hands in pockets, asked, 'Do you know where I might be able to get a dinner jacket?'

SEVEN

Miss Devonshire, cool and immaculate, strode into Central Control and leaned down beside Max's chair.

The room had a muted, orange glow at this time of night, with just a minimal staff of five operatives at the consoles below the curved wall of screens.

'Which Oculator do you have the casino on?' she asked.

Max nodded. 'Screen Seven,' he said. 'Magnify, please.'

The screen in front of Max and Miss Devonshire blossomed into life, showing the opulence of the Aura Casino three levels below the ShopZone. Balconies with gaming tables were rapidly filling up with elaborately costumed guests, while chandeliers glittered in the soft red light.

'Is everything ready?' she asked in her soft, husky tones.

He didn't look up at her, but smiled. 'Everything's ready.'

She came over to him, and stood beside him. 'You still have your doubts, Max.'

He didn't look at her, but shivered a little. 'You know my position, Elizabeth. I don't like it, but I'm interested in what you have offered me. That's why I'm doing this. The *only* reason.'

She pouted a little. 'For Barbados. For your retirement. Yes, Maxie-waxie, I believe you. You're the misguided, honourable man. Well, if that's how you want to play it…'

He turned and glared at her, annoyed. 'Look, I don't really care about your creepy employers, or their dodgy morality. I work for Sir Gerry, and he's a decent man. And all I know is, what I've been offered is a once-in-a-lifetime opportunity. You may not appreciate that, Elizabeth, because Daddy owned land and sent you to a private school.'

She sighed, put her hands on her hips. 'Playing the poor little English guy card again?'

'It's not a *card*,' said Max irritably. He turned away from her again, pretending to survey the screens so he didn't have to look at her. 'I thought I'd wasted my life. But now look at me. My father would have been proud of me for making Carson Polymers a success.'

Miss Devonshire laughed. She put her face up close to Max's and spoke very quietly. 'Carson Polymers,' she said, 'was just one more tin-pot company going to the damn wall. You'd be nothing without me, Max. *Nothing*.' She drew back from him, nodding in satisfaction. 'Just you remember that.'

Max Carson didn't answer.

But his eyes were cold and resolute.

Shaneeqi looked around the glittering Aura Casino at all the people who had come to worship her.

Ruched curtains fell at intervals, in great shimmering

waterfalls of velvet, from high above the balcony where Shaneeqi stood. They fell past the thronged gaming balconies and down to the chequered dance floor below. Six huge, glittering chandeliers hung suspended, catching the subtle red lighting and reflecting it. Soft classical music played in the background. On the floor far below, white-gloved waiters and waitresses circled smoothly and discreetly, dispensing flutes of champagne and elegant canapés: twists of filo pastry stuffed with salmon and herbs, melt-in-the mouth triangles of crispbread and caviar, tiny globes of melon hand-rolled in crunchy bacon.

Shaneeqi, amused, watched the whirl of air-kissing and embracing, the flouncing of frills, the twirling of canes and the tottering on high heels. She caught odd snatches of conversation. 'I just *had* to come here,' said a tipsy young woman in a short red dress, who was also sporting red fingernails and red heels. 'Hyperville is just so wonderful, it's like a dream come true. I broke my credit card out of the ice-block to be here.' Her circle of admirers chortled jauntily. The guests, in flamboyant costumes from throughout the ages, milled, chatted and laughed. The casino was rapidly filling up.

'I want something discreet,' Shaneeqi had told the Hyperville people, 'but kind of ostentatious at the same time. I know you'll get it right.' And they had. It was as if they had read her mind.

If there was one thing Shaneeqi loved in life, it was being Shaneeqi.

She hadn't always been, of course. She remembered when she had been plain old Shannon Eyam. The girl whose teachers had told her she was stupid and that she'd never add up to much. 'It's no good thinking you're going to be a pop-star, Shannon Eyam,' her headmistress had said to her sternly. 'You need to be thinking about qualifications. Getting a proper job.' But Shannon hadn't left school with any qualifications worth speaking of – and employers hadn't been falling over themselves for someone with a D in Food Technology and an E in Leisure and Tourism. She hadn't been allowed to take Music, which she knew she was good at, because of 'timetabling problems'. So she'd spent two years on the dole, hanging round the estate, smoking and causing low-level trouble.

But then there had been Ted, the youth worker, who'd seen something in her and got her organising activities with the disaffected kids. Then, that same year, the Lottery money had come through for a new youth centre with its DJ-ing and recording booth – and Shannon Eyam had really started doing something with her life.

She sang and DJ'd in clubs for a couple of years. Then she went up for *Sing It* on one of the cable channels, and got into the final ten. She was noticed by a sleazy producer – she soon got rid of him – and then by a good guy, Mike, who was cool and wanted to be her manager. And things slowly took off. A download first, a retro white-label pressing next, club gigs up and down the country with the material she and Mike had been writing – songs, real songs with a dash of techno and R'n'B – and then it had happened. Shaneeqi was suddenly in demand. 'Overnight sensation', they called her in the press, although she knew it was so much more than that, and harder work than they made it seem.

The touring was a killer. City after city, hotel room after hotel room, one tiny radio studio after another with DJs who hadn't really listened to her work and didn't really know who she was. She was starting to wonder if it was all worth it when she'd met Paul Kendrick at a charity do, just after he'd split up with his long-term girlfriend. And they clicked, just as her career went stratospheric. One million downloads for her third single, huge advance orders for the *Shaneeqi In Blue* album, a sixteen-date European tour.

On the balcony, he slid soundlessly beside her, slipped an arm around her waist. 'All right, babe?'

She smiled up at him, leaned up for a kiss. 'Yeah. Great.'

'You were smiling. Thinking about something nice?'

'Just the old days. How I can't believe this kind of stuff is really happening.'

Paul smiled again. 'Yeah. Tell me about it.'

'I'm looking for that girl,' she said. 'The one who helped me earlier. Katy, I think she was called. I want to give her something. Dunno what – some tickets or something.'

Paul nodded absently. 'Tell the guys. They'll sort it out.'

'I will.' Shaneeqi peered over the edge of the balcony, looking at the milling hordes of the party below. She leaned up and kissed her husband again. 'Shall we go and circulate?'

Paul winced. 'I ain't really any good at that sort of thing. You go. I'll come down in a bit.'

'All right. And tell me if you see that girl,' she said. 'Katy, she's called. Or Kate, I think. Oh, and...' Shaneeqi waggled her Hypercard at him. 'Can you order us some more champagne?'

'I will, babe.'

He watched her go, and smiled as he plugged the Hypercard into the slot in his phone.

***

The Doctor was busy.

He hadn't come to Hyperville by accident, although he hadn't exactly told Kate about this in great detail yet. He thought he could trust her, but he'd known her less than a day – and, sometimes, humans reacted badly to information overload. Kate seemed good, though. Sharp.

He walked through the vast, colourful ground floor of Fashionista, which was becoming quieter for the evening shift. He was holding his liminal sub-wave energy detector, careful to keep the compass-like object close to his chest whenever he passed the rotating eye of a camera.

Hyperville never closed, but there was always a lull between the dedicated daytime shoppers and the midnight rush. This was the time when the staff managed to snatch quick breaks, and take a breather, a time when the pace and rhythm of the place slowed a little, with the evening murmur only occasionally punctuated by the beeping of cash-tills.

The Doctor turned in a full circle, watching the needle of the detector wobbling. 'Hmm,' he said. 'Inconclusive.'

He narrowed his eyes at the nearest display, consisting of three female dummies in artful dance pose, shiny black plastic limbs draped with diaphanous white material. He flipped his glasses on, peered at them, trying to get as close as possible.

A young store assistant, blonde and burnished, sidled up to him.

'Are you interested in the Muses range, sir?'

'What?' The Doctor turned to face her for a second, looked her up and down. 'Er, no, no. Just looking.'

'For a lady-friend, perhaps? We have some excellent deals on at the moment. Ten per cent off with a phone-linked Hypercard. Muses clothing is eco-centric, ergonomic, intimately shaped to fit whatever form. It's the clothing of the future.'

The Doctor grinned. 'No, no, I've seen the clothing of the future. It's not that great. Really. Not much different from today, to be honest. You know. Shirts, trousers, skirts, blouses… the odd tie. Sometimes a *very* odd tie.'

The girl smiled nervously. 'Right…'

'Oh, yeah. Well, OK, in about sixty years, PVC comes back with a vengeance. And it gets a bit rubbish in the mid-twenty-second century when the 1970s are in again. Actually, in the twenty-third as well, to be fair.' The Doctor took his glasses off and looked thoughtful. 'But no, mostly you can't go wrong with a classic look.' He peered at the mannequins again. 'I'm interested in these dummies. What are they made of?'

'Sorry?' The girl looked taken aback. She was obviously not asked this question very much.

'It's important. Really, very important. Do you think I could get a sample from one of them? Just a scrape off the hand, or a bit of hair, or…' The Doctor saw the girl looking nervously from side to side. 'No? Oh, all right. I suppose not.'

'It's Plastinol,' said the girl nervously.

'I'm sorry?'

'Well, everything's Plastinol, isn't it? These days. Practically everything, anyway. It's the latest stuff. You can make just about anything out of it.'

The Doctor smiled. 'Thank you. That's very useful.'

He shoved his hands into his pockets, and remembered the specimen jar with the Doomcastle vampire's tooth in it. He needed to check that out. With the TARDIS impounded – and he wasn't going to waste time trying to track it down right now – he needed somewhere else.

'So I can't interest you, then?' said the girl hopefully.

The Doctor tilted his head to one side. 'Tell you what,' he said. 'I'll come back tomorrow. See if it's still in fashion. See you!' He hurried out into the mall, dodging the late-night shoppers and keeping a close eye on the Oculator bouncing high above the crowd.

The Doctor was looking for an internet café – and it didn't take him long to find one, up on Level Seven, among the fake trees and fountains of Hilton Boulevard. The computers, sleek and silver, had a Hypercard slot on the side of the monitor, but a quick, discreet burst with the sonic screwdriver got one up and running.

The Doctor tapped enthusiastically at the keyboard for a bit, keeping an eye on the staff. When it became apparent that nobody was really interested in what he was doing, he rummaged in his pockets and unloaded a pile of electronic equipment onto the desk in front of him.

'Now then,' he muttered. 'Bit of jiggery… and maybe some pokery…'

'Intruder detected,' Tess called into her wrist-communicator, as she flipped the hatch open and heaved herself up into the WinterZone. 'In pursuit.'

'Do *not* damage it, Miss Tilbrook,' snapped Max Carson's voice in her ear. 'The rogue unit needs to be preserved and reprogrammed. Do you understand?'

'Yes, sir.' Standing amid the fake snow, Tess nodded to her team of two men and two women. 'Ready? Let's go.'

They ascended a steep bank of snow, boots holding the slippery ground firmly, and emerged beyond the treeline. The white expanse below the glittering starlit dome was empty

– Tess had already used her authority to close it off to the public. On the ridge, she put infra-red binoculars to her eyes and scanned the landscape.

Down in the hollow, Santa's Grotto stood quiet and empty, a small wooden cottage festooned with flashing lights and shiny tinsel. The guardian snowmen, which would normally have welcoming arms out and eyes shining brightly – in a way Tess had to admit she found slightly sinister – were now dull and silent, standing like plump white statues.

And then she saw a flash of movement – pink in the darkness.

'There!' she said, pointing. 'Fan out. You two, across the ridge that way and intercept. You and you – with me.'

Tess pounded down the slope, followed by the two guards she had designated.

The Shaneeqi party was in full swing.

The Doctor and Kate descended the illuminated staircase towards the black-and-white chequered floor – Kate nervously, the Doctor with his usual insouciance.

Kate had a good look at the crowd as they came down into the hall. Beneath the sparkling chandeliers, guests circulated in a whirl of genres, styles and epochs. Women in eighteenth-century silk dresses and ornate masks laughed with men in sharp, twenty-first-century designer suits. A couple in matching white-leather outfits and thin ties, looking very 1980s, were chatting happily to a group of Goths in elegant lace and full white make-up. On the far side, near the bar, she saw a crowd of girls in little red-and-black catsuits and matching devil-horns, as if dressed for a hen-night, laughing uproariously at some joke.

A smattering of guests had dressed formally, like the Doctor and Kate, in dinner jackets and modern designer ball gowns – most of these were trying their luck at the gaming-tables staffed by smartly red-waistcoated croupiers. Pounding synth-pop music bounced around the room, hammered out through invisible speakers above the babble of voices and laughter, and the air was scented with vanilla and cinnamon.

'Quite some party,' said Kate.

'Mmm.' The Doctor was unenthusiastic. 'I've seen better.'

'Hello, darling,' said a tipsy red-haired woman in a red dress and red high heels. 'Don't I *know* you?'

'Um, I don't think so,' said the Doctor nervously, looking her up and down. The fingernails were red, too.

Kate was amused. 'Girl in every port, Doctor?'

The woman shrugged. 'It doesn't matter,' she said, quaffing a large gulp of wine. 'That's not a designer jacket.' She prodded the Doctor. 'You're *cheap*,' she added disgustedly, and staggered off.

'Um… how… did it go with Sir Gerry?' the Doctor asked, wrinkling his nose and trying to pretend that encounter had not just happened.

'Rhiannon's out,' Kate told him, nervously adjusting her elegant silk dress.

'I'm sorry?'

'Well, you know, he fired her. It's his little thing. He sort of points his finger at you and says *You're out!* I think he didn't like her attitude. He told us all to give our initial impressions of Hyperville's strengths and weaknesses in thirty seconds, and I think Rhiannon was just a little *too* spot-on. Then he went off in one of his helicopters to a meeting in London. Seriously, Doctor, *did* you know that woman?'

'*No*! Oh, look!' The Doctor nodded in relief to the white-jacketed, white-gloved waiter who had arrived, soundlessly, at their shoulder with a tray of wine glasses. 'Hello.' He took a glass and sniffed it. 'What year is it?' he asked.

The waiter remained impassive. '2013, sir.'

'Ah. No, no, I don't mean literally what *year*. Although, to be fair,' he added for Kate's benefit, 'I do often ask that. I mean what year is the wine?'

The waiter sighed and raised his eyebrows. '2013, sir,' he repeated, with just a hint of condescension.

'No, I... oh. Oh, I see. Thank you.' The Doctor took two glasses and handed one to Kate. 'So what about you?' the Doctor murmured, as they stepped forward and blended into the crowd. 'Presumably you didn't tell Sir Gerry what you really thought?'

'Give me some credit, Doctor.'

'And he's not rumbled you yet?'

'Not as far as I know.'

'Good – ooh, look! It's the Little Eye again.' The Doctor nodded upwards, and they saw an Oculator bouncing above the party guests on its little blue jet of gas. It spun round in a full circle, scanning the entire room.

'Won't Mr Carson be watching you on that?' Kate asked.

She still wasn't sure if associating with the Doctor was going to get her into trouble, but she knew it was the only way she was going to find out the truth about Hyperville.

'I hope so. As long as he can see where I am, he won't get suspicious.' The Doctor smiled, raised his glass at the Oculator.

'Suspicious?' said Kate.

'Mmm. Yeah. I was a little bit naughty earlier on. I accessed

Hyperville's new Central Program and did a little poking around. They intend to bring it online at midnight.'

'How did you do *that*?' she asked, amazed.

The Doctor scratched his ear. 'Well, I cross-matched the resonance codes with the initiation software, and introduced an induction loop into the—' Kate was glaring at him, her arms folded and her eyebrows raised. 'OK, OK. I... waved a magic wand.'

She grinned. 'See? Keep it simple and everyone's happy.' She nodded to the stage at the front of the casino hall. 'Look out! Madam's going to address her people.'

Shaneeqi was at the microphone. The room fell expectantly silent. Behind her stood the entourage which Kate had seen earlier, hands on hips in their classic pose: the two pale, besuited young men, the two muscular men and the woman in mirror-shades with flowing, silvery-white hair to her waist.

Kate glanced up at the Doctor. He was staring intently at the entourage, his glasses on, leaning slightly forward. She narrowed her eyes at the stage. There was something very stiff and formal about the way the entourage was standing, she thought. Maybe that was what they were paid to do.

'... great moment in my career,' Shaneeqi was saying. 'I'm really, really grateful to you all for coming and supporting me like this.'

The Doctor had his energy detector out again. 'Something's wrong,' he muttered.

Kate saw that the needle on it was still oscillating wildly from left to right. At her shoulder, an immaculate, gloved waitress topped up her champagne glass, but Kate hardly spared her a glance.

'What does it *mean*?' the Doctor murmured.

'And now,' Shaneeqi said, giggling, 'I want to let someone very special have a few words. He's my rock, my partner, my other half… Ladies and gentlemen, please give a very big hand for Mr Paul Kendrick!'

The room erupted into loud cheers, with many of the guests actually jumping up and down. A woman on Kate's right, one of the crowd in eighteenth-century dress, waved her pince-nez in the air like a football rattle.

'Who's he again?' the Doctor whispered to Kate, as Kendrick, eyes covered with shades, strode on to the stage with a big wave.

Kate tutted. 'Goldenball Paul! The England captain!'

'Right.' The Doctor sounded none the wiser. 'Hang on a minute…'

Kendrick was at the mike, his rather thin voice with its South London twang at odds with his tanned, burnished physique. 'I just wanna say, it's great to see my wife's talent being recognised by somewhere like Hyperville. Somewhere that'll be a place for future generations to come and see what, y'know, the biggest and best of the twenty-first century really looked like.'

'He's deluded!' muttered Kate.

The Doctor was staring at his energy detector. The dial had stopped spinning. It was pointing forwards, at the stage.

Kate glanced down at it. She looked back up at the Doctor. 'Does that mean… ?'

The Doctor tried to shove his way through the crowds of revellers in front of him. 'Everybody!' he shouted. 'Get down! *Quickly!*'

For a second, Kate was unsure what to do.

Then she saw Shaneeqi, standing at the edge of the stage, looking bemused. She grabbed the girl's hand and pulled her down behind a table by the fire exit. All around them, other revellers were dropping uncertainly to the floor behind the roulette tables and the bars.

She saw Paul Kendrick looking accusingly at the Doctor.

'You, mate,' he said. 'I want a word with you.'

The crowd suddenly parted, leaving the Doctor isolated in an expanse of dance floor.

'Um,' he said. 'Right.'

Paul Kendrick smiled.

'Mr Carson told me you might be trouble, Doctor,' he said. 'Seems he was right.'

Miss Devonshire smiled. In the dimness of the control centre, it seemed as if her eyes were glowing a dull green.

'Activate it,' she said. 'Activate it *now*.'

Max Carson's hand hovered over the main console. For a moment, he looked up at her.

'I want the entire, exclusive world rights to Plastinol,' he said. 'With no room in the contract for wiggle room.'

She rounded on him, eyes harsh and angry behind her glasses.

'You have Barbados, Max. Now just do it.'

Max's finger stabbed down on the button.

A blaring, staccato siren began to echo repeatedly through the whole of Hyperville.

Deep, deep below the lowest official level of Hyperville, in the darkness of Level Zero, the pulsing green Consciousness thrashed and glowed, as if it had received a burst of new life.

A sound echoed through the great space – it could have been a howl of triumph, or even a screech of pain.

Out in space, the cluster of rough spheres moved ever closer.

They pulsed with a greater intensity, now, as they skirted the gravitational pull of the great planet Jupiter.

They knew where they were heading.

Kendrick extended his hand towards the Doctor. He pointed straight at him.

His eyes glowed pinkish-red.

The crowd had fallen back, leaving a space around the Doctor. He backed away, though his natural curiosity was, as ever, fighting his fear.

There was a clunking sound from somewhere within Kendrick's arm. A dark line began to form across his fingers, along the joints.

'Oh, dear,' the Doctor said softly. 'Should have seen this coming.'

With a fleshy, slurping, unzipping sound, the front half of Kendrick's fingers fell away as if on a hinge, revealing the dark tube of an alien gun barrel buried inside his wrist.

Shaneeqi put her hands to her face and screamed.

EIGHT

'This is Hyperville. This is a security announcement. Please make your way to the nearest exit. Please note, this is an official security announcement. Please make your way quickly and quietly to the nearest emergency exit. Do not stop to collect shopping or other items. Thank you.'

Reece thumped the wall of the hospitality suite for the fifteenth time in as many minutes. Despite the Doctor's request, they had still somehow ended up here.

'Did you hear that alarm? What are we *doing* in here? We need to get out and find Mum and Derek!'

Chantelle, feet up on the coffee table, was painting her nails. Unlike her restlessly pacing brother, she looked calm and collected. 'Just calm down, bruv. I'm thinking.'

'Oh, right.' Reece folded his arms and scowled. 'Hold the front page.'

'Things are going belly-up. And they don't want us to know about what we've seen, right?' said Chantelle carefully.

'Right.'

'But that Doctor bloke. He knows what's going on. We've got to find him somehow. Get a message to him.'

Reece slumped onto the leather sofa and gestured around the bare but tastefully decorated suite. 'And how exactly are we gonna do that?' he asked.

'Like I said – I'm thinking.'

'They ain't exactly given us the Freedom of Hyperville,' Reece said, nodding at the electronically locked sliding doors to the lounge. 'I dunno about you, but I've not noticed many other ways out.'

Chantelle looked up, smiled and returned to her nails.

'Thinking,' she said again.

Captain Tess Tilbrook crested the ridge at a run and, controlling her breathing, scanned the snowy landscape with her binoculars.

'Nothing,' she murmured. 'Dammit – either it's gone or it's very good at hiding.' She spoke into her wrist-communicator. 'Unit One, report please?'

The voice of one of her team crackled back at her. 'Nothing here, Ma'am. We've checked the grotto and the WinterZone Garden.'

'Unit Two?' said Tess.

The response came quickly. 'Nothing in the forest this end, ma'am. Just heading to the ice lake.'

'Be careful,' said Tess. 'Remember, Mr Carson wants it alive.'

Over the years, Tess had learnt not to ask too many

questions of her employers. Her job was to provide a secure, safe environment for the punters to spend money in happily – and that had sometimes meant doing things she wasn't happy with. Things like doubling the armed patrols on the prestige shops of Xenophon Boulevard, because there had been a terror threat, and having to look mean and moody because the circumstances demanded it, and querying anybody who looked vaguely suspicious.

She didn't always like her job. But it was a job. And that was something to be thankful for.

Her boys, Joel and Barney, always said, 'Be careful, Mum,' when she went off to work. It had become a bit of a standing joke.

These days, she knew it wasn't so funny.

And suddenly, she noticed it had become very cold in the WinterZone.

Properly cold.

Tess shivered. The temperature was always kept a little lower than the rest of Hyperville, just so the punters felt they were getting the true WinterZone experience. But this was different. She could see her breath. She could feel it in her fingers and toes.

There!

A flash of movement in the trees.

Tess dropped to one knee, shouldered her gun and fired. The shot went wide.

She was sure she heard a quiet, childish cackle coming out of the trees.

'Units!' she snapped. 'Target intercepted. Forty degrees north of my position. Block off its retreat!'

Tess, her breath aching in her lungs, pounded towards

DOCTOR WHO

where she had seen the thing. A homicidal homunculus, the Doctor had said, she remembered with a shiver.

She ran, pounding the snow, past the tree which her stray shot had punctured. She was trying to turn, sweep the gun in a wide arc, just in case the thing doubled back behind her.

There was a *blizzard* whipping up.

It was impossible, but it was happening.

Although it was convincing, Tess knew the snow was just very small mass-produced flakes of the new substance, Plastinol. She didn't know they actually had a way of making it 'snow' inside the Dome. *And where the hell was that back-up?*

There was a soft *flump* sound from behind her.

Tess whirled round.

Standing on the white-covered path in front of her, framed in the whirling snow, was a small girl in a pink-and-white striped jumper, a red hat and red trousers, and red wellington boots. Her face was shiny, smiling. It had a strangely waxy quality, as if polished or moisturised.

Tess levelled the gun.

'All units,' she said quietly and calmly into her radio. 'Target located. Please assist.'

The girl smiled.

She started to advance on Tess, through the whirling snow.

'You will stop walking,' Tess said calmly, feeling her heart pounding. She spoke to the child just as she'd always tried to speak to Joel and Barney when they were being naughty. Images of the boys' faces flashed into her head, scenarios from the past: mud or cereal trodden into the carpet, milk spilt on the DVD player, toys all over the hall. *You will clean that up. You will tidy that away.*

The child advanced, fingers flexing. She lifted her arms as if to run to Tess for a hug.

The cold, harsh snow whipped up into a fountain around Tess and began to cling to her.

And then the child cackled. It was a harsh, electronic sound, like the noise a cheap doll might make.

'*Stop! Walking!*' Tess yelled. She could feel the Plastinol snow clinging to her face, getting into her mouth and nostrils. It tasted cold, clammy, bitter.

The child leapt at Tess, eyes glowing.

Somehow, Tess dodged it, spinning round, and the child smacked against her shoulder as it leapt, falling to the ground. It rolled like an athlete, righting itself again almost instantly, snarling.

Tess fired.

She unleashed bullet after bullet into the small creature. They smacked into it, plopping as if into soft mud, ripping holes in the waxy flesh and in the dummy's coat and trousers. The dummy's head, ripped away, hung hideously and grotesquely off the neck.

Smoke dispersed.

The hot, angry smell of the incinerated bullets and plastic wafted through the chilly WinterZone.

The dummy was lying on its back in the sizzling snow.

Tess, hands tight on her gun, didn't dare breathe. She reached out, her hand drawing nearer and nearer to the bullet-riddled dummy.

The dummy sat up.

Tess, gasping, took a step backwards.

And then the holes closed up.

One after another, as if they had not been there, sealing

with a slurping, squelching sound, as if it were made of dough or porridge. And then the head flipped back on like a bin lid, and twisted back into place.

The dummy-girl made an odd sound, rather like retching. It leaned forward, coughed up the spent bullets and spat them into the snow.

Its eyes glowed brightly again, and it cackled.

Horrified, Tess threw her useless gun at the creature, and turned to run.

She couldn't. She felt panic overwhelming her.

The Plastinol snow had crept up round her boots and was holding her in place with the strength of concrete. Like a living thing, it slurped and crawled up her legs. The flakes which had already attached themselves to her face suddenly swept together, formed into a saucer-sized, living mass of snow, clogging her mouth and nose and stopping her from crying out.

The dummy-child, whose plastic body now bore no sign of the bullet-wounds, cackled again, reached out its arms and stalked forward.

And then it jumped onto Tess, its small plastic hands tight around her neck.

'Down!' The Doctor shouted. 'Everybody get down!'

He looked in horror at the four members of Shaneeqi's entourage, expecting that they would get to their feet at any moment and level their deadly fingers at the party guests in the same way.

But to his surprise, amid the general screaming and sounds of breaking glass, they threw themselves to the floor and covered their heads along with everyone else.

Above their heads, high in the ceiling near the chandelier, the Oculator buzzed and swooped like a giant silver insect.

There was a loud crash, the sound of several objects dropping in unison, and the tinkling of broken glass.

The Doctor looked wildly around. He couldn't see Kate.

What he did see was that each one of the catering staff had dropped their tray of champagne or canapés, and that every one of them – the black-gloved waitresses and the white-gloved waiters – was pointing, as if accusingly, at a group of revellers.

As he watched, the gloved hands each clunked, then opened in unison with that same fleshy, slurping sound – revealing dark, metallic gun barrels built into the hands.

The Doctor slowly raised his hands. 'Autons,' he murmured. 'All Autons. *Why* didn't I work that out?'

Paul Kendrick, smiling, circled the Doctor, his gun-arm close to the Time Lord's head. 'These are newer models, Doctor. Enhanced Autons. Some of the exhibits, which you managed to do some damage to, are older units. Ready for replacement.'

The Doctor tried not to move as Kendrick circled him. 'So. Right, hello. Golden boy of English football. Don't know much about football. Sorry… An Auton facsimile. No wonder you never missed a penalty. Well, I assume. How did you pass the medical?'

Kendrick chuckled. 'People in authority are easily bribed, Doctor.'

'I see.' The Doctor's voice had lost its flippancy. Through clenched teeth, he said, 'Let these people go. I don't know what you want, but you can't *possibly* need them.'

'We are already letting hundreds of people go, Doctor,' said

Kendrick quietly. 'Can't you hear it?' The sound of the klaxon blaring was not relayed as far down as the casino, but it could be heard in the distance, echoing through the upper levels. 'We're clearing Hyperville. With the exception of a small number of humans whom we… require.'

'Require?' The Doctor wasn't sure he liked the sound of that.

'Yes, Doctor. Autons, like any tool, need to be tested. Calibrated. Trained. They need to be aware of the nature and speed of human responses.' Kendrick nodded to the nearest Auton-waitress, and stepped aside.

She stood, booted feet apart, in front of the Doctor, and he heard the buzz and the whine as her gun-hand powered up.

Both his hearts thudded furiously. He was wondering how to get out of this one.

The Auton-waitress swung in an arc away from the Doctor and fired at the nearest table.

A ray of harsh, incinerating crimson whipped across the room, seeming to tear the very air apart with its intensity, and blew the table and chairs into glowing fragments. In the haze of light, they turned red, then white, and dissolved before the pieces hit the floor. A acrid smell of burning drifted through the room.

One of the gamblers, a man dressed as an eighteenth-century pirate, swooped on the Auton with a chair in his hands, holding it high above his head, ready to bring it down on her.

'No! Don't!' the Doctor yelled, but it was too late.

The Auton-waitress swivelled as if on a pivot, and blasted the guest and the chair with the same hot, red light.

He didn't even have time to scream. He and the chair

hung suspended in a crackling haze for a microsecond. They turned red, then blazed white, before dissolving into white-hot globules which were scattered far and wide across the dance floor.

Paul Kendrick nodded. 'Thanks,' he said to the Auton-waitress.

She retracted her gun – the barrel snicking back, the fleshy hinge closing up with a slurping, zipping sound as if it had never been there – and stood with one hand on her hip, still as a statue.

The Doctor moved forward, propelled by anger, but Kendrick held up an admonishing gun-hand. 'No, Doctor.'

'That wasn't *necessary*.'

'Perhaps not. I'm sure nobody else will be as reckless.'

'What do you *want*?' the Doctor asked furiously, his teeth clenched. 'What's all this about?'

'To the lift, please, Doctor. You, it has been observed, have particular knowledge. Mr Carson and Miss Devonshire have… a proposal for you.'

'What kind of proposal?'

Kendrick's pale face flickered in what could have passed for a smile. 'You'll find out if you come with us.'

'I'm not coming,' said the Doctor firmly. 'Not unless you let all these people go.'

'Hyperville is on lockdown,' said Kendrick. 'They're not going anywhere. Not ever.'

The Doctor opened his eyes wide and stared hard at Kendrick. 'Then neither am I,' he said.

For a long moment it looked like an impasse.

Kendrick put one hand to his ear, as if perhaps receiving orders. The Doctor was sure he heard a clicking sound. Then

Kendrick nodded, and lifted his arm up high. 'Why don't you all run?' he said in a quiet voice, as if making a polite suggestion.

The party guests all stared at him.

The Doctor's eyes narrowed.

For a split second, he wondered why Kendrick didn't just fire into the crowd straight away.

Then Kendrick's wrist-gun exploded into a jagged beam of crimson light, which smashed into the Oculator. The blast blew it into sparkling, fiery chunks which glowed and vanished, fizzing into the air as they pirouetted downwards.

People screamed, scattered, pushing and shoving as they headed for the exits. Clutch-bags, mobile phones, pince-nez, headdresses, chairs, tables, wine glasses and canapés were scattered and kicked aside in the rush.

'*Run!*' Kendrick shouted again, and his narrow eyes lit up with a fiery red, as if illuminated by bloodlust. His arm swivelled down, pointing at the retreating back of one of the slowest guests, a young woman in a bright purple bodice and ruched silk dress.

'No!' the Doctor yelled, and cannoned sideways into Kendrick, knocking him so that the beam went wide, hitting the chandelier. The Doctor bounced off Kendrick and rolled over.

The glass was hazed with a corona of red light, then exploded outwards like a shower of glass droplets. They turned red and then white as they fell, like heavy, slow-motion rain, towards the room. Before they hit the chequered dance floor, they fizzed and crackled and disappeared in mid air. The room was filled with a sharp, acrid tang.

Kendrick staggered to his feet. He swung round, and

his face wore a sneer. His gun-hand pointed straight at the Doctor, who was being hoisted to his feet by two of the Auton-waitresses.

'Come with us,' said Kendrick softly.

From behind the fire door, Kate and Shaneeqi had watched with a mixture of horror and anger.

'I don't understand,' Shaneeqi hissed. 'My husband... what's he *doing*?'

'I don't know if that's really your husband,' Kate said uncertainly. 'The Doctor said these... Auton things can make facsimiles. Copies, of people.'

'So where the hell is *Paul*?' Shaneeqi snapped.

'I don't know. But we're not going to get very far by charging in there. It won't help the Doctor, or anybody else.' Kate pulled Shaneeqi's arm. 'Come on. I've got an idea...'

Reece and Chantelle looked up as the sliding door to the hospitality suite slid open.

Two dark figures were framed in the doorway. Chantelle felt her stomach plummet. Instead of the security men they had been expecting, two figures in suits stood there.

They looked bizarrely like wedding guests, thought Chantelle. The man wore a steel-grey suit with a purple silk tie and gleaming cufflinks. The woman was in a grey silk skirt and jacket and shimmering mauve blouse, with an elaborate corsage in her buttonhole and a leafy, purple fascinator adorning her hair.

And they were not human.

As the figures stepped into the light, Chantelle saw with horror that they had the smooth, plastic faces of the display dummies from one of the megastores. Light glinted off their polished black skulls and their eyes glowed red.

Reece backed off, holding his hands up. 'Whoa. This better be a joke,' he said.

The two dummies strode forward in unison. They raised their hands as if to point accusingly at Reece and Chantelle.

Some instinct made Chantelle realise she had to duck. She grabbed Reece, and pulled him behind the sofa – just as two sizzling bolts of light ripped through the air where they had been standing, hitting the far wall. A chunk of the wall turned red, then white, then exploded into a crackling cloud of dust, which disappeared before it hit the floor. A sharp tang filled the air – it smelt like vinegar, thought Chantelle, or window-cleaner.

The dummies turned one way then the other, seeking their prey. As if sniffing them out.

'What the heck *are* they?' Reece hissed.

'I dunno.' Chantelle was thinking frantically. 'We've got to get out. Warn the Doctor. He'll know what to do.'

'Yeah,' said Reece. 'Not disagreeing here. But – slight problem!'

There was another sizzle, a burst of heat and a *whoomph*, and half the sofa disappeared, as if disintegrated into hot droplets by some intensely powerful weapon. Fragments of the sofa were splashed against the wall, where they dripped like liquefied wax for a second before dispersing.

Chantelle was frantically turning out the contents of her bag. Lipstick, tissues, mobile phone… None of it seemed any use. Then her hand closed over a small bottle. *Of course*, she thought. She drew it out thoughtfully and tucked it into the top pocket of her shirt.

'Reece,' she whispered. 'Do exactly what I say. Right? Gimme your penknife.'

Reece did. 'What are you gonna do?'

'This,' she said. She leaned out from behind the sofa. 'Oi!' yelled Chantelle. 'Dummies!'

She hurled Reece's penknife against the wall, where it hit with a loud crack. As the little silver knife fell to the floor, both the dummies turned and blasted it with incinerating beams.

Reece looked horrified. 'That was a present from Grandad!'

'I'll buy you another!' Chantelle snapped. 'Now – stay here!'

And, head down, Chantelle charged *towards* the dummies.

She knew, as she ran, that it was the stupidest thing she had ever done in her life. But something was pushing her, something was telling her it was right. She could smell the burning wood and foam of the sofa, and the nasty, sweetly plastic smell of the shop-window dummies as they twisted towards her.

Chantelle leapt onto the back of the female dummy and gripped its head, feeling it thrash beneath her.

She'd expected it to feel cold to the touch, but it was horribly warm and clammy. She could see the male ducking from one side to the other, trying to get a clear shot.

And then she pulled the bottle of nail varnish from her pocket, jammed it up against the dummy's head and poured. Right into its eyes. Glutinous, purple streams covered the dummy's polished face.

Nothing seemed to happen at first. It was thrashing back and forth, its strength unabated. Chantelle could feel it about to throw her off. Her feet and hands lost their grip and she was hurled against the door with a juddering impact that knocked the breath from her, making the room spin. The bottle of nail varnish rolled away. *Where the hell was Reece?*

The dummy swivelled round to face Chantelle. Its hand pointed straight at her.

'Oh well,' Chantelle said. 'Worth a try.'

The dummy's eyes glowed, and its gun barrel snicked fully from its wrist.

Chantelle screamed and covered her face.

The blaring alarm rang through the empty halls of Hyperville.

A disc formed in the floor of Afrika Plaza, beneath the great illuminated, suspended globe.

It emerged from the floor, becoming a cylinder of glass, packed with Shaneeqi's party guests in their motley costumes from various eras. Several of them were hammering in panic on the curved doors of the lift. Finally, it opened – and they ran, scattering across the Plaza, some leaving feather boas and shoes and scarves in their wake.

The Plaza was no longer empty. From the floors above, dark figures began to drop, screaming and screeching with hellish voices.

The witches.

The party guests panicked, confused, some of them recognising the Doomcastle synchro-thesps and feeling terrified and unsettled by seeing them out of context.

On the other side of the Plaza, a trio of armoured knights clanked and crashed, sweeping wildly with their halberds, crashing into plants and knocking over the flower stalls and sweet displays.

Screams went up from the crowd.

They ran in different directions, looking for exits from the Plaza. Some even ran for the lift, but a jittery bolt of light from one of the witches' fingers smashed the glass cylinder into a million pieces, which dispersed into sizzling white droplets.

The majority of the party guests were running into the one available exit, down the tree-lined Kennedy Boulevard, towards the Megashop exit.

One of the witches fired after them, a sizzling bolt of light enveloping a woman in voluminous skirts as she ran.

Bolt after bolt crackled from the witches' fingers, slicing through the air and scarring the marble floors.

Glass shopfronts splintered and melted, droplets of glass splashing and sizzling and congealing on the floor. Pungent, green smoke filled the halls like fog from a blasted heath.

The Oculators bobbed above the massacre, watching.

NINE

In Hospitality Suite Nine, the dummy staggered. Its shining nose and mouth suddenly cracked, bruising and shrivelling like rotting fruit, and the surface split. The plastic of its face puckered and hissed like the skin of boiling milk, black froth erupting from its eyes and mouth.

Chantelle uncovered her face cautiously, watching the delayed effect of her nail-varnish-bomb. She watched in fascination and horror. The nail varnish had seeped inside it and was beginning to take effect, she realised.

An unearthly screech echoed through the room as the dummy bent over sideways, clutching its frothing head, black foam dripping down its clothes and collecting on the floor.

Chantelle saw Reece. He had scooped up the bottle.

He threw it straight at the other dummy, hitting it square in the face. The tough glass bottle didn't smash, but it did splatter the mannequin with purple nail varnish. The effect seemed even faster with this one. The liquid bit into the plastic, making it split and froth. The dummy screeched, staggering backwards, throwing both arms out wide, fists clenching and unclenching as if in pain.

Chantelle rolled over and sat up.

The dummy fell to its knees.

And then its head exploded. It burst with a wet, squelching sound like a soft fruit.

Liquefied black plastic splashed across the carpet and the coffee table, leaving a steaming, gaping hole at the dummy's neck. Its arms flailed wildly like those of a puppet, and then it crashed forward, hitting the carpet in a cloud of noxious, oily black steam.

Coughing and choking, Reece and Chantelle staggered from the suite, Chantelle hit the closing button and the door swished shut.

They looked at each other.

'Seriously,' Reece said. 'You put that stuff on your *nails*?'

Chantelle, getting her breath back, grinned and leaned against the wall. 'Course.'

Reece shook his head. 'You're weird.' He looked up at his sister with new admiration. 'How did you *know*?'

She grinned. 'Bit of guesswork. And GCSE Chemistry. Listen in class, that's my tip.' She glanced up and down the corridor. 'Come on. I think this place is about to go to hell.'

Reece didn't move.

'Reece, I said come on.'

'I want to know what's happened to Mum,' he said. 'This place… it's bad, isn't it?'

Chantelle put her hands on his shoulders. 'Trust me, Reece. The Doctor's the key to what's going on here. If we can find him, he can help us find Mum again. Now let's get out of here.' She turned to go. 'Sorry about your penknife, by the way,' she added.

Reece shrugged. 'Like you said. We get out of this, you're buying me another!'

On Level Zero, the lift doors rumbled open.

The Doctor looked around, impressed by the huge, echoing, freezing cold space. It was like a kind of underground warehouse, he thought, but also reminded him of a cathedral with its vaulted arches and dark pillars.

Paul Kendrick emerged first, followed by the two Auton-waitresses with their gun-arms trained on the Doctor. The Doctor noticed that, unlike the two waitresses, Kendrick had breath which misted in the cold air.

Kendrick waited by the lift as the waitresses escorted the Doctor the length of the warehouse-like space, footsteps echoing up into the darkness, and then he got back into the lift again. The Doctor wondered briefly where he was going.

Miss Devonshire and Max Carson were waiting at the far end.

'Hello!' the Doctor said, nodding. 'Mr Carson. We meet again. Still got the little beardy thing going on.' He tutted. 'I'd lose it if I were you. It's very 1990s.' He turned to Miss Devonshire. 'We've not met, have we? I'm the Doctor.'

He extended a hand. She kept hers clasped together.

'I am aware of you,' she said with a smile.

The Doctor shrugged, let his hand fall back to his side. 'Nice place you've got here. Well, nice-ish. Bit chilly.'

'Indeed,' said Miss Devonshire levelly.

'I don't suppose you've got any tea? I'm dying for a cup of

tea. An Earl Grey with a dash of milk. Not too much milk. Just a dash.' He nodded at the wall behind them. 'And a lovely piece of warp-shunt containment technology. Now, I wonder why you've got that there? As if I didn't know.'

Inside its translucent plastic bubble, the Consciousness thrashed and glowed, as if it recognised the Doctor.

Miss Devonshire, hands clasped neatly in front of her, walked slowly towards the Doctor, her heels clicking. She raised her eyebrows behind her austere rimless glasses. 'Quite finished, Doctor?'

'For the moment. If you like. Right, is this the bit where you tell me all about your plans and say the information won't be any use to me, because I'm "about to die"?' The Doctor made finger-quotes in the air. 'Because, you know, I *really* like that bit. I'd better take notes. Could I sit down?'

Miss Devonshire folded her arms.

'That tea would be good,' the Doctor went on. 'And some shortbread. Those chunky round ones. With the... little thistle stamped on them.' He gestured with his hands, describing the shape of the biscuit. 'I *love* the little thistle.' He looked up hopefully.

'Quiet,' said Miss Devonshire.

'Oh.' The Doctor looked disappointed. 'Can't you even manage a *hold your tongue, Doctor, or I shall remove it*? That's one of the best ones I've had,' he added to himself.

'Max,' said Miss Devonshire wearily. 'Tell him.'

Max Carson glowered at the Doctor. 'You are familiar with the Nestene Consciousness?'

The Doctor grinned. 'Oh, that old thing. Yeah, defeated it three times now. Or four. Actually, could it be five? I lose track.'

'We're not asking you to defeat us, Doctor,' said Max. 'Not even to fight us.'

'Really?' The Doctor looked surprised. 'Now, that *is* interesting. What hold have they got over you, Maxie-boy? And how much does Sir Gerry know about this?'

Max smirked. 'That old fool doesn't know anything.'

'Thought so. Just checking.' His expression flicked from facetiousness to cold, hard anger. 'What do you want from me?'

Max looked at Miss Devonshire for confirmation. She nodded.

'You seem like a man who knows about extraterrestrial technology,' suggested Max.

The Doctor shrugged, attempted to look diffident. 'Well, a bit.'

'Warp-shunt interfaces,' Max said. 'This unit fell to Earth thirty years ago. The physical manifestation of the Consciousness was, ah, damaged, injured almost irreparably. It's taken thirty Earth years of slow recuperation, but it's almost there.'

'Could I look?' the Doctor asked softly.

Max nodded, and gestured for him to come forward.

The Doctor crouched down, both hands on the softly glowing, translucent green bulge. 'All right,' he murmured, 'let's have a listen…'

Reece and Chantelle were running through the strangely deserted Megastore. The escalators were still running, rumbling away to themselves in an uncannily efficient manner. The huge shop floor showed evidence of having been hastily abandoned, thought Reece – some shelves had been tipped over, and clothes from the racks strewn on the floor. As they ran, Chantelle was scrabbling at the shelves, filling her capacious handbag with as much nail varnish and hairspray as she could get her hands on.

'That's *stealing*!' Reece said.

'Got any better ideas?' she snapped. 'What if we see more of those plastic goons on the way out? What are you gonna do? Talk nicely to them?'

Reece didn't have an answer. OK, he thought. Stick with Chantelle. I know I hate her sometimes, but she is my sister. And we need to get out of here.

They emerged into the mall at a skittering pace, and paused for breath. Nobody was to be seen in either direction. Hyperville was unnervingly quiet. Above them, high in the Atrium, the Oculator still bobbed on its little jet of gas. Some things didn't change, thought Reece.

'OK,' Chantelle said, looking up and down the empty, echoing mall. 'This is Hyperion Boulevard. There's an exit just round here. C'mon! We need to find Mum. And the Doctor!'

They ran – past abandoned flower stalls, cafés and shops – and rounded the right-angled corner, then skidded to a halt.

They had expected to see the great, glass doors emblazoned with the three-circle Hyperville logo at the end of the mall. Instead, tough-looking steel shutters covered the glass from marble floor to vaulted ceiling, blocking out the light from outside.

Reece stared at the steel shutters in horror. 'Now what?' he cried.

'Back. Come on.'

They turned the corner – and saw two women running down the escalator towards them. One was dressed in a business-suit and glasses – should have been smart, Reece thought, although she was looking like she'd been pulled through a hedge backwards. The other, a thin and bony girl, had dyed-red hair, a psychedelic top and black leather trousers.

Reece recognised her, but his sister had got there first.

'Shaneeqi!' exclaimed Chantelle in amazement.

Shaneeqi and her companion stopped at the foot of the escalator. The two pairs regarded each other with suspicion, backing slightly away from one another.

'We ought to get the Doctor,' Chantelle said uneasily.

The woman in glasses looked startled. 'The Doctor? You've seen him?'

'Not for ages!' Reece answered. 'Have you?' Then he shook his head. 'Hell, never mind you. It's Shaneeqi! Can I touch you?'

The young pop-star held her hands up. 'Just… don't,' she said.

The other woman spoke softly. 'She's had a very trying day. She's just found out her husband's an Auton.'

'A what?' Reece said.

'Big walking dummy-thing made out of plastic?' Chantelle offered. 'Paul Kendrick's one of *those*?'

Shaneeqi nodded, folding her arms and looking away.

'I could have told you that after some of the rubbish free kicks he took,' Reece muttered.

'I'm Kate Maguire,' said the woman. 'Do you kids have any idea what's going on here?'

'The place evacuated,' said Chantelle. 'Dunno if everyone got out.' She nodded behind her. 'Someone's sealed us up.'

'Blast doors,' said Kate, nodding. 'They've got blast doors!'

'What?' Reece looked confused.

Kate tutted. 'Urban environments, terrorist protection. Basic stuff. Someone, somewhere, hit an alarm and the blast doors closed. We're sealed in. No way out.'

'Oh, great,' said Reece. 'You're trying to think, hey, maybe things aren't that bad. Maybe it's just a few malfunctions, or whatever. And then someone goes and says something like *no way out*.'

Shaneeqi whirled round, crouching. 'What was that?'

Kate, Reece and Chantelle stared at her. 'What?' Chantelle asked.

Reece licked his lips nervously. He hadn't heard anything.

'Down there,' said Shaneeqi softly, nodding.

The party of four stared down the length of the mall. The empty boulevards, shops, megastores, restaurants and cafés were hauntingly still and quiet.

'There's nothing,' said Reece. 'You must have imagined it.'

He turned in a full circle, just checking. Everything seemed quiet. No... there was something odd about the glass window of the vast Gladrags store, to their left. It was *shimmering*.

'The boy's right,' said Kate. 'We're getting jumpy. Come on – the Doctor needs our help.'

Reece stared at the blue-tinted window of Gladrags. Shapes were moving behind it. He was mesmerised by the rippling effect on the tinted glass.

'No,' he said. 'Hang on.'

The window burst open.

It didn't smash – it was as if had suddenly been made fluid. It *bloomed* outwards, making a shimmering, round shape festooned with droplets of glass, like a slow-motion replay of a stone dropped into water.

The Autons kicked and punched their way out of the liquefied glass.

The glass hit the floor with a smack, hissing, steaming and starting to solidify again.

They were shop-window dummies of all sizes, in various colours of plastic, adorned with cutting-edge and everyday fashion: jackets and trousers, sparkly summer dresses, school uniforms, casual T-shirts and beach shorts, sunglasses, underwear. They were staggering, feeling their way as if blind. There was even, Reece noticed with a sick sensation, one of those mannequins deliberately made with no head, so that it looked like a reanimated, decapitated corpse. It whirled around, its stubby neck bobbing back and forth, fleshy plastic hands clenching and unclenching. Fragments of semi-molten plastiglass window clung to the dummies.

Reece stared in horror and clutched Chantelle's arm.

'Hang on,' Kate was saying. 'Look. They're still confused, *look!*'

The way the Autons moved was oddly, unsettlingly like that of drunken human beings. They tried to walk in straight lines but lolloped, staggered, arms held out in front of them as if needing support. One or two of them bounced off each other or hit the shop windows, shattering them.

'How much of that stuff did you pick up?' Reece asked his sister, not daring to take his eyes off the Autons.

'Not enough to dispose of this lot,' she muttered.

Kate looked at the teenagers. 'What stuff?'

Chantelle showed her the contents of her handbag. 'Anything with the right chemicals in. I offed a couple earlier with nail varnish.'

'Are we gonna run or not?' Shaneeqi screamed.

They all, for some reason, looked at Kate.

'OK, run!' she said.

They ran, heading for Europa Plaza. Further down the mall, another window burst open in the same way – liquefied, as if something had happened to its molecular structure. And then another, and another.

Both behind and in front of them, windows exploded outwards in showers of fluid droplets, a sloshing, glooping noise echoing up into the vaulted ceiling of Hyperville as Auton arms and legs slashed and thrashed their way out.

Shopfronts were shattering all along the mall.

They kept running. Reece's heart was pounding.

And then several small, pink shapes started dropping from the balconies above them.

The four humans skidded to a halt. Reece stared in horror.

Each of the pink shapes hit the floor with a squelching sound, flexing its little limbs. Then more, and more.

Facing them was a small army – two dozen or more – of life-size baby dolls. The kind, Reece realised with a sick feeling, that he had bought for his little cousin Sadie just the other year, when she was a toddler. They were dressed in a variety of baby clothes: pink gingham caps and tunics, or frilly red-and-white dresses, or acid-green romper suits.

They weren't even cute, Reece thought – their rigid, pink faces with glaring blue eyes and unnaturally red mouths just looked evil to him.

The one at the head of the crowd raised both its hands.

'*Hug me, Mummy!*' it said in a tinny, gurgling voice.

The others raised their arms in unison, following its lead.

Two dozen squeaky, inhuman doll-voices echoed through the mall. '*Hug me, Mummy!*'

And then, as if controlled by a single mind, the dolls put their little feet one in front of the other.

With arms outstretched and blue eyes open wide, and faces fixed in rictus grins, they began to advance on the humans.

The Doctor was still examining the containment unit inside which the green, glowing form of the Consciousness slumbered. Its actual form could not be seen that clearly behind the frosted, translucent material of the pod. There was sometimes a hint of a thrashing tentacle, sometimes a shadow which could have been a claw. Now and then a flashing, tentative imprint would be made against the material of the pod, like the mark of a misshapen hand on cold glass, before whatever protuberance had made it was snatched away again.

'Your thoughts, Doctor?' asked Miss Devonshire.

'Physical manifestation for the Consciousness,' the Doctor murmured, 'isn't defined in the same way as you or I would define our bodies. It's more than just a brain in a casing of flesh. It's more of a… *concept*.'

'Go on,' said Miss Devonshire, smiling.

'It can exist in various forms, various places, various times even. It exists within everything it controls. The basic shop-window dummies, the more advanced Autons with the firepower like Suzanne and Joanne here.' The Doctor nodded to the two immaculate, black-gloved waitresses. 'Then the facsimiles, like your mate Georgie-Best-boy upstairs – and this.' He nodded to the translucent pod. 'Kind of like the heart. Only not the heart, necessarily. Could just be the appendix. Or the duodenum. Depending how you define it.'

'A little muddled. But basically correct, Doctor,' said Miss Devonshire quietly.

The Doctor pulled a stethoscope out of his pocket and listened. 'Ahhhh… Okaaaaay…' He stood up, hands in pockets, and turned to face Max and Miss Devonshire again. 'And the one thing which unites all its various manifestations is a molecular structure with a close affinity to what, here on Earth, is called *plastic*. Polymers of high molecular weight, some partially amorphous. All here in Hyperville in abundance. All of which makes me wonder… why this manifestation is actually *dying*.'

Max and Miss Devonshire looked at one another, then back at the Doctor again, who leapt down from the platform, walked up to Miss Devonshire and all around her.

'May I?' he asked, extending the stethoscope.

She spread her hands. 'Be my guest.'

The Doctor listened to Miss Devonshire's chest – first on one side, then on the other. Then he pulled a face, flipped his glasses on and peered intently at her face. 'Who *are* you, exactly?' he murmured.

She smiled. 'My name is Elizabeth Devonshire. My parents came here from the USA in 1976. I am, shall we say, one of the key players in the setting up of Hyperville.'

He shook his head. 'Ohhh, you're far more than that…'

'Elizabeth?' Max asked. 'What does he mean?'

She did not answer. 'Go on, Doctor.'

'Tell me about Hyperville.'

'What is there to tell?' She spread her hands. 'A glorious empire of consumerism on one site. A place for the organics to shop, to play, to be entertained.'

Max looked curious. 'Organics?' he said.

'She means humans,' said the Doctor coldly. 'Human beings. That's what I prefer to call them.'

Miss Devonshire smiled. 'A place for the organics – the *humans* – to *congregate*. Despite your meddling, Doctor, there are still approximately a hundred human units at large in the complex. My Autons will find them. They will destroy some. Others will be kept for our... training exercise.'

'You've had a few problems. Or rather...' The Doctor nodded towards the Consciousness. 'It has. Damaged, disorientated... It can't control all of the Autons properly, can it? That's why you've had rogue units. Couple of weird sisters, some knights, a manic train driver. Not to mention the murderous little one. Where *is* the little one?'

'We're working on it.'

'And what do you want me to do?' asked the Doctor, circling her and taking off his glasses.

'I want you to fix the signal,' she said quietly. 'Amplify it.'

'Amplify it?' said the Doctor cautiously. 'What for?'

'The distress signal that this unit has been sending out is to a Consciousness spearhead cluster located at the fringes of your solar system. This unit needs to attain escape velocity in order to realign with the cluster, and then it can locate a new breeding ground. If a suitable one is found, then the people of this paltry, messy planet which you seem to love so much will be left in peace. Never bothered again by the Nestenes.'

'And if I don't?' the Doctor asked carefully.

Miss Devonshire turned her head towards him and smiled. 'Then I shall release the Autons from Hyperville, and they will kill every organic on this planet.'

TEN

The young woman from Shaneeqi's party, the one in the red dress who had proudly defrosted her credit card, was running down Kennedy Boulevard, looking in horror at the shattered shops.

She didn't really understand what had happened, but she knew Hyperville would never be the same again.

Where was she going to shop now?

She had taken off her beloved Jimmy Choos and couldn't bear to let go of them, so she was holding them as she ran, along with the bottle of champagne she had liberated from the party. Her dress was ripped at the shoulder and her hair tousled.

Then, she skittered to a halt.

Two shop-window dummies were marching determinedly towards her.

She stopped, blinked. She took a deep swig from the

champagne, plonked it down on a nearby bench and spread her hands.

'Oh, *guys!*' she exclaimed. 'Come on!' She fumbled for her credit card and her Hypercard, offering them to the Autons in desperation. 'Look!' she said. 'Look, I can pay you. It's all on credit, but I pay off the minimum every month, I swear, please, you can have whatever you want—'

Babbling, she backed up against the wall as the two Autons continued to march relentlessly towards her. Her eyes bulged in fear.

'Please!' she begged. 'You guys! I came here to shop! I *live* to shop! You've got to let me—'

The Autons stopped.

She laughed nervously, spread her hands, shoes dangling from one, credit cards from the other.

'OK,' she said. 'Right. Can we talk? Let's talk!'

The Autons, as one, lifted their arms.

Their hands opened with a fleshy slurping sound, followed by two simultaneous clunks.

The girl's face fell.

'Oh, come *on,*' she said.

Both Autons blasted her at the same time, the fizzing sound echoing through the mall and the ultra-bright, incinerating light of their weapons flashing off every reflective surface.

The girl was slammed back against the shop window.

Suspended in mid air, she rippled in a vortex of red light, then white. Then she, her shoes and her credit cards burst into a shower of hissing, white droplets.

It was as if she had never existed.

'What the flamin' 'eck is going *on* in this place?'

The dolls in Hyperion Boulevard turned, as one, little pink feet squelching and stamping, little red eyes glowing in anticipation of new prey.

'Sir Gerry!' cried Kate, her voice filling with hope.

The Chief Executive, briefcase in one hand and cigar in the other, stood amid the debris in the shattered mall. 'Kate?' he said. 'What's happened? I go away for three hours and come back and a bomb's hit the place!'

'Who's that guy?' asked Chantelle.

'The head honcho,' said Kate. 'The big cheese.'

She glanced behind them. The disorientated Autons who had emerged from the shops were looking as if they were gathering strength. At their feet, the dolls, chattering and chuckling quietly to themselves, were reaching out their little arms in apparent delight.

'Whatever we're going to do, guys, can we *please* do it quickly?' Shaneeqi snapped.

'OK…' Kate tried to think on her feet.

Sir Gerry looked down in horror at the army of baby-dolls. 'Is this some new line Max has been developing? They look like ugly little blighters.'

'Blighters.' Kate looked up suddenly. 'Blighters, *lighters*… Sir Gerry! Give me your lighter!'

'What?' Sir Gerry looked confused as the dolls began to fan outwards, some stomping towards him and others heading for Kate, Shaneeqi, Reece and Chantelle.

'Your *lighter*, Sir Gerry! Your cigar lighter!'

Sir Gerry, backing away from the advancing dolls, fumbled in his pocket and threw the lighter over to Kate, who caught it smartly in both hands.

'Give me that hairspray,' she said to Chantelle.

The girl handed the canister over. 'What are you going to do?'

'Something clever,' said Kate, 'with any luck.'

Kate wasn't at all sure that what she was going to do would work, but she remembered seeing something similar in a film about invading alien bugs once.

She pressed down on the aerosol, and at the same time clicked Sir Gerry's cigar lighter on so that the spark caught in the flammable stream.

The rush of flame almost made her drop the thing, but she kept her finger down on the aerosol.

A wave of fire hit the dolls, scorching the heads of those in the front rank. They scattered like ants from an upturned anthill, and Kate was sure she heard an unearthly screeching sound coming from the red mouths.

'Come on!' Kate yelled to her astonished companions. '*Run!*'

The full-sized Autons, firmer-footed now, were already stalking down the mall towards the conflagration.

Kate clicked the lighter and the aerosol again, giving the dolls another burst.

She caught three of them in the same cloud of orange fire, and felt the intense heat as their heads and upper bodies liquefied in front of her, drops of molten plastic splattering the marbled surface of the mall floor like pink wax. The pungent, toxic smell of melting Plastinol filled the mall, and an evil whitish-green smoke emanated from the melting dolls.

Kate grinned, breaking into a run with only a glance over her shoulder. 'That's what you get for being made of plastic!' she yelled, and ran after the others with a whoop.

***

The Doctor looked at Miss Devonshire and raised his eyebrows.

'Oh, well,' he said. 'If you put it like that… Give me access to the warp-shunt drive software.'

Miss Devonshire gestured to her laptop, on a table next to the platform. 'All yours, Doctor. But no tricks. Or we begin.' She nodded to one of the Auton-waitresses, who stalked over to Max Carson.

The Doctor watched curiously as the Auton reached out for Max's arm. He could see the expression of puzzlement on Max's face as its tough, flexible plastic fingers clamped down on his arm, and saw the puzzlement turn to fear as he was slowly forced to his knees.

'We will begin with Mr Carson,' said Miss Devonshire quietly, 'now that he has outlived his usefulness.'

Max looked in horror at her. 'Miss Devonshire,' he whispered. He licked his lips. '*Elizabeth*… We had a deal. We had an arrangement.'

She perched on her chair, legs crossed elegantly, and smiled. 'From which you have profited handsomely. But ultimately, Max, you are just another organic.' She gestured to the Doctor. 'I suggest you begin.'

They burst through the nearest fire door, Chantelle first, followed by Reece, then Shaneeqi, then Sir Gerry, puffing and wheezing, and finally Kate, bringing up the rear.

Kate checked behind her. Those dolls, she thought in panic, could move fast. She'd had one when she was a little girl. Little Miss Sleepy-Eyes, she was called. You pulled a string at her back and Little Miss Sleepy-Eyes said, 'I love you, Mummy.' She had always been envious of her friend Rebecca

Tomlinson who'd had the i-Doll, the one with the chip in it which said several hundred different combinations of things. Envious up to a point. But the i-Doll was, in many ways, even spookier. It was so real, its eyes moist and blue and its soft plasticky flesh warm and lifelike. Kate had been happier with the plastic artificiality of Little Miss Sleepy-Eyes.

And now there were several dozen of them, marching towards the fire door they had just come through, arms held out, eyes blazing red.

'How many of these things are there?' Shaneeqi gasped, leaning on her knees to get her breath back.

Kate tried to stay calm, focused. 'The Doctor said this Consciousness thing could tune itself into plastic. Like it's part of it.'

'Oh, great,' said Chantelle. 'So we need to be afraid of *everything*. Think about it.' She pulled her mobile phone out of her pocket, held it on her palm and looked at it warily, as if it were a rodent sitting there about to bite her.

Kate grinned. 'You mean you're not already?'

Chantelle glowered at her.

'What's through here, Sir Gerry?' Kate asked, nodding at the maintenance door ahead of them.

He looked up, arms folded, and surveyed the number above the maintenance door. 'Wild West World, love. Sealed off. Routine maintenance.'

Kate walked up to him and glared at him. 'Then let's get it open.'

Sir Gerry looked confused. 'Why would we want to do that, you daft lass?'

'Because,' said Kate patiently, 'it's just possible the Autons won't think of looking for us there. OK?'

Sir Gerry narrowed his eyes for a moment, then he clamped his cigar back between his teeth and growled with approval. 'Good thinking,' he said. 'Now, if I can just remember the code…'

'Hurry up,' said Chantelle. 'Please,' she added with a quick smile.

Sir Gerry peered at her over his glasses. 'This sort of thing can't be hurried, young lady. Hyperville has a very sensitive security system!'

'*Hug me.*'

Kate whirled around. She could hear them, on the other side of the fire door, scratching at the metal.

And then the slamming began.

Kate stared at the thick fire door.

About half a metre above the ground, it was starting to buckle like wood.

'Sir Gerry!' she yelled.

'All right, love, keep your hair on!' He sighed, leaning over the keypad. 'I'm sure they changed the combination last week…'

A gash appeared in the metal fire door. A small pink fist punched its way through, and a second later one of the dolls, its eyes glowing crimson, tore its way into the lobby, ripping the fire door like paper, and poised to spring.

Reece grabbed the fire extinguisher and stepped forward. 'Right!' he yelled. 'I'll get this one!'

Kate tried to stop him. 'Reece, no!'

He hurled it at the doll. The pink creature went sprawling, its head squashed cartoon-like into the shape of a frying pan. Then it somersaulted and, with a stomach-churning *pop* sound, its head squished back into its former shape again.

And then it launched itself at Reece, knocking him off his feet, little pink hands clutching at his neck.

Horrified, Kate tried to go and pull the doll away from him – and felt her feet give way from under her as two other dolls, which had just come through the gap, grabbed her ankles and pulled her downwards.

Chantelle and Shaneeqi were pinned against the far wall, a line of dolls between them and the others.

Reece, choking and clutching at the doll which was pinned to his neck, began to turn purple…

'Well, Doctor?'

He looked up from the tangled mess of wiring which he had pulled out of a panel in the wall next to the pulsing pod in which the form of the Consciousness was contained.

Miss Devonshire stood there, hands on hips, booted feet planted firmly apart, eyebrows raised above her rimless glasses.

'Well…' The Doctor shrugged, pulled a face. 'There's some limited friction on the internal drive circuits. A bit of wear on the directional warp-shunt vectors, a touch of decay in the anti-bumping coagulant. And the gravity compensation diodes? Where *did* you get those? They've really seen better days. Apart from that, it's fine.' He straightened up, tapping his chin with his sonic screwdriver. 'But that's not a problem, is it, Miss Devonshire?'

She put her head on one side. 'What do you mean?'

'Because you don't want it to be able to get into space again. You don't want to use the warp shunt to get the Nestenes to a new breeding colony. No, what you want from the warp-shunt core is its raw *power*.'

Miss Devonshire's eyes were cold and hard. 'Just do it, Doctor.'

'Oh, no, no, no.' The Doctor started pacing up and down. 'You must think I'm stupid. You must think I'm Mr Thick from Thicksville, Thickasee. You see, I know a little bit about computer networks. And earlier on, before Shaneeqi's party, I had a little root around in your Central Program.' He stopped pacing, grinned at Miss Devonshire.

'Elizabeth!' Max Carson groaned desperately. His wrist was turning white where the Auton-waitress gripped it.

She ignored him. 'Explain yourself, Doctor.'

'And not only did I have a little root around,' the Doctor said, 'I put a little extra of my own in there. A little trigger. You see, I like to talk, Miss Devonshire. I talk a lot.' The Doctor strode over to her laptop.

'Stop him!' she snarled.

The Auton-waitress dropped Max, who sprawled on the floor, and started striding towards the Doctor.

He leaned in to the microphone. 'I talk a lot, and I often talk a lot of *rubbish*!'

The screen flared green.

The gentle green light inside the pod became an incandescent, harsh whitish-green, and the Autons, clutching their heads, staggered around in inelegant pirouettes. Miss Devonshire's mouth opened in silent horror.

And then a sound began to issue from the Consciousness itself, a deep, angry scream as if torn from the pits of hell, like the sound of shearing metal mixed with the screeches of demons.

The doll attaching itself to Reece suddenly sprang off, as if pulled by an invisible thread, and smacked against the wall. The dolls clutching Kate slackened their grip too, just as Sir Gerry got the internal door open.

'Come on!' Kate yelled.

They piled through the door. Kate went through last, pulling the door hard behind her. She was sure she heard a thump as the little bodies hurled themselves against the metal, and she wondered how long it would hold.

Feeling heat on her back, she turned round.

It was as if she had walked straight into a sauna – the heat and humidity were unbearable. The other side of the door from which they had emerged appeared to lead into a ramshackle wooden barber's shop surmounted by a red-and-white pole. Blinking, Kate shaded her eyes and looked around in what she told herself had to be artificial sunlight. She could smell dust, and wood, and could see a dry street lined with wooden buildings and lamp posts stretching out in front of her. A crudely painted wooden sign on a pole read 'Welcome to One Horse Town'. She could see other signs in blocky lettering swinging eerily in the light breeze. They said BANK and ASSAY OFFICE and SHERIFF on one side, while on the other the buildings proclaimed themselves to be MA'S PLACE, the SHOOTERS' SALOON and the GUN STORE. There was a distant sound of chirruping cicadas.

Hills and rocks clustered in the bright distance, peppered with spiky cacti. Behind the buildings was a battered rail track, leading to a station at which the wooden Hyperville Train with its bright blue locomotive could be seen at rest – driverless for now.

Kate knew straight away what look they were aiming for here – the clichéd, Western-movie version of an American frontier town, looking exactly the way people expected it to because this was what they had seen hundreds of times before. Whether any of it was accurate or not was totally beside the point. It was pretty convincing, she thought – this part of Hyperville must have cost millions.

Sir Gerry wiped his sweating brow with a spotted handkerchief. 'No idea,' he said, 'how much we lost through having to close this Zone down. It was one of our biggest attractions.'

'Are we sure they're not gonna get through?' Chantelle asked worriedly, backing away from the barber's shop.

'That door's reinforced dura-titanium, lass,' said Sir Gerry with grim satisfaction. 'One thing to thank Health and Safety for.'

Kate stood, hands on hips, and surveyed the landscape. She felt the angry prickle of sweat under her armpits, and would have been uncomfortable but for the fact that Sir Gerry, Reece and Chantelle looked equally drenched. Only Shaneeqi was managing to look pale and cool, and had slipped a pair of shades on.

'You all right, Shaneeqi?' Kate asked awkwardly.

'Fine,' she said, in a small, distant voice. Her shades made her eyes unreadable.

Reece and Chantelle looked awkwardly at one another.

'OK. We can't keep running,' said Kate. 'We need to fight back. Chantelle – tell me about that little armoury in your handbag.'

Sir Gerry sighed. 'I need a drink,' he said, nodding towards the Saloon.

'You won't be able to get one, will you?' asked Chantelle interestedly. 'Not a real one?'

Sir Gerry chuckled. 'Don't you bank on it, m'dear. I know the tricks of this place, don't forget. Come on!'

The SherwoodZone was silent and deserted. A dim, reddish light shone through the artificial trees, making it look as if the foliage had been steeped in blood. The Marian-bot and the Robin-bot lay inert where they had been left in the clearing.

There was a rustle in the undergrowth, and two contrasting figures stalked out. Paul Kendrick, immaculate in his designer suit and tie, looking almost human again but for the faint red glow in his eyes.

And beside him, the one Max and Miss Devonshire had referred to as Beta-4 – the plump, sinister toddler-Auton with the blonde hair and glossy black face.

Their eyes were sweeping left and right, scanning every centimetre of the forest.

'Find all the remaining organics,' said Kendrick in an emotionless voice. 'All organics within the perimeter zone must be eliminated.'

Beta-4 turned her head to look up at him, and her rigid dummy-face creaked, her plastic face stretching into a smile. The low chuckle emanated from deep within her again.

'Program adjustment for appropriate emotional responses? Excellent,' said Kendrick with grim satisfaction. 'In other words, Beta-4 – I think you're enjoying this.'

The Doctor tapped out a sharp rhythm on the keyboard.

He glanced up. Miss Devonshire and the Auton-waitresses were on their knees, clutching at their heads as a screaming, whining noise echoed through the chamber.

The Doctor smacked his forehead with his hand. 'Oh, no,

no, no. Hang on. That's induced an overload. I didn't align the parameters correctly!'

'Step away from the keyboard.'

It was one of the Auton-waitresses, speaking impassively with the voice of the Consciousness, her wrist-gun levelled unsteadily at the Doctor.

'Ah. Suzanne. Or is it Joanne? Won't be a moment.'

'Step away from the keyboard!'

'Or what? Or you'll kill me? If you want to kill me, why *haven't* you killed me, Suzanne? Aha!' The Doctor grinned. 'You're frightened you might damage something. Powerful digit you've got there. Packs quite a punch. Tell you what… How about we overload the overload?!' The Doctor punched a key with panache. '*Cowabunga!*' He looked disconcerted. 'I don't believe I just said that.'

The pod flared with light.

The Autons staggered, and Miss Devonshire turned towards the light, as if drawn to it magnetically.

For a moment the Doctor seemed uncertain. Then he took a decision, and started running for the lift.

Max looked from the Pod and Miss Devonshire to the Doctor – then, as if deciding in an instant where his destiny lay, picked himself up and ran after him.

The Doctor aimed his sonic screwdriver at the lift-call button, his feet pounding on the floor. As he reached the far side of Level Zero, the loud *ping*! announcing the lift's arrival echoed through the vast space.

The doors slid open and the Doctor threw himself inside.

Max followed, rubbing his injured wrists.

The Doctor did a double take. 'You?'

Max nodded, gasping. He pressed himself against the other

side of the lift, watching the Doctor warily. He was no longer the suave vision of calm that had first appeared to the Doctor – now, his collar was loose, his tie was askew and his pale face was slicked with sweat.

The lift doors slid shut, cutting off the hideous screeching, and the lift began to ascend.

The Doctor nodded to Max. 'OK. Nicely done,' he said. 'I always thought you'd be the type to save your own skin… By the way, I don't mean to be personal, but you *really* need a good antiperspirant.'

Max sneered and drew his slim, silver pistol. 'You're going to get me to Sir Gerry's helipad, Doctor. That's the only way out of this madhouse now.'

'Oh.' The Doctor, hands in pockets, looked a little disappointed. 'I was hoping for a little more humility. Something along the lines of, thank you for saving my life, Doctor. Yes, I see you're right, now, Doctor. No good can come of consorting with the Nestene Consciousness, Doctor, no matter how much money they offer me. Sorry, Doctor… No? Nothing like that? Don't you even want to know what I did?'

Max shook his head. 'Some kind of audio-triggered virus, I expect. Does it matter?'

The Doctor grinned. 'Well, yes, it does. Because it hasn't done any damage. Not seriously. Just gave them a nasty migraine while I thought of the next stage in my plan. Give them thirty minutes. Miss Devonshire will pop the Nestene equivalent of a couple of ibuprofen in, and they'll be away again. And then we really will be in trouble.'

'Why?' asked Max cautiously.

'Because they'll be really, really miffed.' He nodded at

the gun. 'And I expect they've got one or two guarding the helipad. So do us both a favour, Maxie-boy, and put the pea-shooter away.'

Carson stared at him for a moment, teeth clenched, sweating.

'You don't really believe all that stuff Miss Devonshire was saying, do you?' the Doctor asked him. 'About finding a new breeding ground and going away and leaving the Earth alone?

'I said I'd help them,' said Max softly. 'Four years, and they've given me everything I needed.' He slumped against the lift wall, but kept the gun trained on the Doctor. 'I was going to retire to Barbados.'

'Been there. Overrated. They *want* this place, Max. They want it because the molecular structure of its plastics and CFCs and oils and artificial gels is brilliant for them. Humans are too imaginative, that's always been their problem. Attracts attention. And this place, it's *perfect*.'

'Perfect?' said Max uncertainly.

'It's like food and a home and a breeding ground all in one. It's the perfect base. They won't leave. They won't leave until they've spread their tentacles out from Hyperville, and turned your planet into Plastic-World.' The Doctor stared at Max. 'Don't you *know* any of this stuff?'

Max tutted. 'The Nestenes are my employers, Doctor. I was almost ruined when Miss Devonshire found me. Have you any idea what it's like to go from success to failure so quickly? From boom to bust? Then an investor comes along and offers to bankroll you for four years. I've got an apartment on the Wharf. Three sports cars. All the designer goods I want.' He grinned. 'Why would I question their motives?'

The Doctor sighed, folded his arms. 'Humans. Nothing ever changes, does it?'

Max stared at the Doctor for a moment longer, as if wondering whether to challenge the comment. Then he made an exasperated sound and pocketed the gun. 'What are you going to do?' he asked.

'What I should have done when all this started,' said the Doctor. 'Get rid of the Autons – and close this place down!' He grinned. 'Cheer up, Maxie. In a week's time you could be lying in your hammock and drinking your light rum and pineapple juice.'

The cluster of spheres, pulsing in perfect unison, had reached the orbit of Mars.

They continued to pulse, and to come closer, sliding effortlessly through space with no visible means of propulsion.

They knew exactly where they were going.

As if they were alive.

ELEVEN

'This is Hyperville.
'This is Hyperville.
'Shop.
'Dream.
'Shop.
'Dream.
'Shop…'

The Doctor burst into the control centre and made a dash for Max's podium. Max followed with a slightly wobbly gait.

Max Carson's heart was pounding. Everything he had thought and believed for the past few years was being slowly undermined. He was starting to think that escape was his only option, and he knew he had to find some way of getting to that helicopter. Barbados. It still had to be an option.

'What are you going to do, Doctor?' he asked.

The Doctor had a quick glance up at the wall of TV screens, but they were nearly all swirling with static. Those which were still relaying images of Hyperville were blurry and flickering.

The Doctor put his glasses on and ducked under Max's console. 'A bit of rejigging of your old CCTV, Max.' He poked his head up above the console. 'Blimey. Not exactly high-definition any more, is it?'

Max shrugged. 'The power's fluctuating,' he said. He wasn't sure if that was the reason, but he guessed.

The Doctor yanked some wires out of a panel under the console. 'Bit of recalibration.' He gave the circuitry a couple of carefully applied bursts with his sonic device. 'Just some fine-tuning. Bad news, Max. You might not be able to get the shopping channel now.'

The screens flickered, and about six of them crackled into sharp relief, leaving the others totally dark.

'Aha!' The Doctor leapt up, grinning and giving the console a thump for effect. He peered in at one of the images. 'Hang on. They look familiar. Where's that?'

'That's Wild West World,' Max admitted. 'We had it sealed off.'

'Because it was dangerous, I assume.' The Doctor sighed, watching the image of Kate, Reece, Chantelle, Sir Gerry and Shaneeqi making their way down the dusty street towards the Saloon Bar. 'Right!' the Doctor exclaimed, spinning Max's laptop round to face him. 'Deal with that in a minute. Central Program, online… let's take a look.'

'What are you doing, Doctor?' Max asked.

'I inserted a trigger-word through one of the subroutines, but they've closed off that access now… *Not* surprising.' The Doctor talked as his fingers flickered over the keyboard.

'Ohhhhh, they're good. They're goody-good-good. Not taken them long to get to grips with the changes in Earth technology... Clever, clever Nestenes.' The Doctor glanced up at Max. 'They've got you pretty much under their plastic thumb. Under their tentacles. Haven't they? Miss Devonshire owns you.'

Max tried to quell the anger he felt. 'I am a man who works for a company, Doctor. Many do worse in the name of capitalism.'

'Still,' said the Doctor, 'I know you've done bad things. I can tell by looking at you.'

Max closed his eyes for a moment.

He remembered Andrea Watson, struggling as the Plastinol spread up her legs from her boots, merging with her skirt, engulfing her in one glossy black tide of plastic...

He remembered giving the order to clear two bodies away from the maintenance tunnels, and for the families of the two men to be told they had died through an electrical fault. Just like the other one...

'Yes,' he said softly. 'I've done bad things. For them.'

The Doctor didn't look at him. 'They always find someone,' he said softly, almost to himself. 'You're not the real enemy, Carson. They are.'

Max opened his eyes. He watched the Doctor work in grudging admiration. 'Who do you work for?'

'Oh, just me.'

'You seem very highly skilled yourself.'

'Phhww.' The Doctor made a modest sound. 'Just experience... You know, when I first met the Nestenes, they were tuned into Seventies retro. Telephones, coloured vinyl, hideous troll-dolls.' The Doctor looked up, stared into the distance for a moment. 'And some really, *really* horrible nylon shirts.' He pulled a face. 'Mind you, I can talk. I used to dress like Jimi Hendrix… Then by the Nineties they'd got to grips with CDs. Do you know there's a hidden track under the sound mix on one of the Spice Girls albums, and when you play it back, it says "The Nestene Consciousness will prevail"?'

Max looked confused. 'They put that in?'

The Doctor looked at him. 'No, no, I put that in. To throw them off the scent. And now, there's so much more plastic-based stuff in the world… so many more ways for them to gain a hold… Aha!' He thumped the space bar with a flourish, baring his teeth in delight. '*Voilà!*'

'What is it?' Max asked.

'The signal Miss Devonshire was talking about. Routed through the TV satellite dish on top of the FunGlobe. Thought as much.'

Max folded his arms. 'I could have told you that.'

The Doctor grinned. 'Yes. But I wouldn't have known you were telling the truth. I don't like you, Max. And I never trust someone who swaps sides at half-time. It's an old trick, and it never gets you anywhere.' The Doctor's eyes suddenly widened as he looked over Max's shoulder. 'Look out!'

Max Carson folded his arms. 'Doctor, if you think I'm going to fall—'

The Doctor hurled him aside as a sizzling crimson bolt cut across the room, smelling like burning metal and smashing into the TV screens. Several of them exploded into crimson droplets. Another blast, and Max's computer had a sizzling hole punched right through the screen.

Beta-4 stood there, her little eyes glowing with malice. And behind her was Paul Kendrick.

'Told you so!' said the Doctor softly, edging a couple of paces away from the burning laptop.

The Auton toddler and the footballer stepped away from the door, heading in separate directions, moving around the control gallery.

Max felt his heart thudding faster.

His hand closed over his concealed pistol.

Something told him this was going to be a decisive moment in his career at Hyperville.

Miss Devonshire was checking readings at the computer. She nodded grimly to herself, then strode up on to the platform and closed her eyes.

'Enough residual power,' she murmured. 'Partly thanks to the Doctor's meddling. The fool! We *can* do it. We *will*.'

She placed her hands flat on the Consciousness's pod. Palms flat against the plastiglass shell, she stood there braced as data pulsed from the central computer into the pod. Inside, the Consciousness screamed, torn apart in pain.

And Miss Devonshire smiled.

Her eyes and mouth streamed with incandescent green light.

The Doctor watched Beta-4 and Kendrick carefully as they circled round the control centre gallery. He was also watching Max Carson out of the corner of his eye. He knew he had no reason to trust the amoral, spineless Director of Operations – and things could still go either way there.

'Hello!' said the Doctor. 'Come for a chat?'

Beta-4 chuckled, and flipped herself along the gantry like a gymnast.

She hurtled hard into the Doctor.

He felt his hearts thumping as his feet lifted from the podium. And together, the Doctor and Beta-4 fell.

The Doctor rolled over onto one shoulder, minimising the impact, but the Auton had righted its small body even more quickly, moving with an amazing fluidity.

There on the control-room floor, with the screens flickering and fizzing behind it, the Doctor found himself looking down the barrel of one small and very deadly wrist-gun.

'*Doctor!*'

He heard Kendrick's voice from the podium above, and looked up.

Kendrick's gun-hand was jammed under Max's chin.

'Don't try to resist, Doctor,' said Kendrick. 'Or things will get very messy for Mr Carson.'

The Doctor slowly raised his hands. 'Sick as a parrot, Mr Kendrick. You've equalised in extra time.' He glanced at the toddler, then up at the footballer again. 'What *are* you, exactly? Because I've got a sneaking suspicion.'

'I am Paul Kendrick,' said the Auton, with a hint of a sneer in its voice. 'I am also the Nestene Consciousness. We are all the Nestene Consciousness.'

'Yes, yes, brilliant. Wonderful self-awareness. But how *long* have you known that, eh? Because you're not a facsimile, are you, Paul? You're not a waxwork or a copy, like the Autons have used before. You're not a dummy like this little lady and her shop-floor friends, or even an enhanced Auton like the Snow Queen and the witches and the knights.' The Doctor raised his eyebrows, and took a careful step forward. 'Ohhh, no. You *are* Paul Kendrick. You're one of a whole new breed of Autons. Miss Devonshire and the Consciousness have been very clever with you – sending you out there, letting you live a life, get married, being a *real person*. Did you know all this, Max? Maybe you did.'

Carson glanced nervously at Kendrick's wrist-gun. He didn't dare say anything.

'And I think,' said the Doctor softly, 'that I know. What's going through your mind. Why you hesitated, earlier at Shaneeqi's party. Why you *stopped*. You didn't kill those people. The Consciousness wanted to kill them, didn't it, Paul? But not you. Not Paul Kendrick, or the vestige in your mind that still *calls* itself Paul Kendrick.'

Kendrick's face was trying to stay impassive, but the Doctor was sure he could read the strain on the super-supple Plastinol visage.

Beta-4 swivelled from side to side, almost jumping up and down in its eagerness to kill. The manic chuckle emanated from deep within its little body.

'Oh, and *you* can be quiet,' said the Doctor. 'It's past your bedtime.' He looked up at Kendrick again. 'Interesting, isn't it, Paul? Can I call you Paul? Paulie?… OK, Paulie's a bit far. Stick with Paul… An Auton who's always thought he's *human*, Paul. Always believed he was. With memories that seem so real, so vivid.'

Kendrick remained impassive.

'I bet you can still smell your school playground, can't you, Paul?' the Doctor went on. 'I bet you can see the face of the first teacher who ever gave you detention. I bet you can remember how the mud felt on your hands after you first kicked a ball into goal. That was, what, twenty years ago? Twenty-five? But it wasn't, was it? All of that was injected into you by the Consciousness when you were born. Just two or three years ago, Paul. None of it ever happened.' The Doctor paused. 'A fake human with fake memories. An Auton who's developing *autonomy*.'

Kendrick's head tilted on one side, and his eyes began to glow threateningly.

'You know it, don't you, Paul?' the Doctor asked. 'Because you've *always* known. There's always been that little hint at the back of your mind, *the suspicion that your memories weren't real*. The streets where you first played football.' He nodded up at Max Carson. 'I expect Maxie's media contacts were able to do a lot. Faking the history, creating a man out of nothing.' He looked back at Kendrick again. 'Kate told me you seemed to come out of nowhere. Because that's exactly what you did. You never existed before. *There was no real Paul Kendrick*. Your entire history, your entire life, is a fiction. But, there, you see, that's interesting. Does it make you any less of a being?'

Breathlessly, the Doctor tried to lock eyes with Kendrick. Staring into that redness, seeing if he could find a way into that Auton soul. There was no response.

'So who are you?' the Doctor challenged. 'Because you haven't always been the Nestene Consciousness. It gave you *memories*, Paul Kendrick. It gave you a personality. A purpose, a life. A talent. And fans! You've got *fans* ! Did you know that? They'll all be there on their little computers, tapping away, comparing your stats from Euro 2012 with those of the past greats. Bobby Robson, Gary Lineker, even Stanley Matthews. Those people, Paul Kendrick, ohhh, they all think you're brilliant.'

Kendrick's gun-arm wavered.

'I mean, yeah, some of them might say you're not as good as you used to be. Trading on past glories. They'd rather watch the videos of your old matches over and over than enjoy the new ones. But you know what? They're wrong. You're still brilliant. Just in a different way.'

Beta-4 clicked and jittered agitatedly. It was obviously waiting for orders from Kendrick, and as yet they were not forthcoming.

'Brilliant,' said Kendrick flatly.

'That's right!' The Doctor nodded enthusiastically. 'And you know what's great about that? Somewhere out there is a child you've given hope to. A child who might not be that good in school, but who can play football like a demon. And they've watched you on TV, and thought, one day, I'm going to be like Paul Kendrick.'

Kendrick's eyes flared a brighter red. 'These things are irrelevant,' he snarled.

'Oh no, not to me, they're not. And not to the thousands of fans. Imagine someone going online and typing in *Paul Kendrick's an Auton*! Imagine if they knew. Imagine if they could *prove* it. Think what that would do to the people who love and admire you!' The Doctor took another surreptitious step forwards. 'Think how it would destroy their world.'

Kendrick's gun-arm came up again, then wavered again.

'They... admire me,' he said softly.

'You are Paul Kendrick,' said the Doctor softly. 'You have a life, you have memories. They may not be real, but the fact that they seem real can make life worth living. And you have Shaneeqi.' The Doctor took another step forwards. 'It doesn't have to be this way, Paul.'

It wavered, then. The Auton which was known as Paul Kendrick. It seemed to take a step backwards and to lower its gun-arm a fraction of a centimetre more.

The Doctor held his breath.

'I am Paul Kendrick,' said Kendrick.

And at that moment, Max Carson ruined everything.

His bony elbow slammed into Kendrick, knocking him off-balance for a second, and then Max whirled round, dropped to one knee and was levelling his pistol.

'Max! No!' the Doctor shouted, but it was too late.

Beta-4 gurgled in apparent delight, swivelling its little gun-arm up towards the podium to try and get a clear shot.

The Doctor charged into Beta-4, knocking the midget Auton over and sending its shot wide. The beam smashed into the screens above, sending globules of dissolving plastiglass raining down like confetti.

Max fired. Six bullets hammered into Kendrick, making him stagger. He lost his footing and plummeted off the edge of the podium, crashing to the floor beside the Doctor.

'Barbados,' he said softly. 'You're not going to take away Barbados.'

But time was up for Max Carson. He was too late for Barbados, or anywhere else.

Kendrick, the bullet-holes in his shirt already closing up, sat up, swivelled his head round and pointed straight up at Max. As if accusing him.

He smiled.

'Sorry, Carson,' he said. 'You're fired.'

The beam hit Max Carson squarely in the chest, hazing him in red, then white.

Max was wreathed in a corona of blood-red, arms flung high, mouth open in astonishment. Then, the image of him, the imprint – whatever it was that remained – fizzed and burst into a shower of droplets.

Kendrick swivelled round and levelled his wrist-gun at the Doctor.

For a second they stared at one another.

Kendrick's eyes flared.

The Doctor didn't gamble. He couldn't be sure that the vestige of autonomy was there any more. He wondered if it had been lost for ever.

He threw himself aside. The beam from Kendrick's wrist-gun slammed into the wall, carving a huge, smoking gash.

Beta-4 chuckled and gurgled.

The Doctor, realising there was nothing he could do, made for the nearby fire door – with a bolt from Beta-4's wrist-gun sizzling within millimetres of his shoulder…

Miss Devonshire felt fully as one again with the Consciousness, for the first time in thirty years.

Little Lizzie Devonshire. Walking through the abandoned warehouses in the bleak, industrial wasteland of this part of Britain.

She didn't know what had brought her there or why. She was running, running past great towering cliffs of warehouses, under looming girders, feet splashing in puddles of foul yellow slime.

She remembered. Running from them. Running from the bullies, from the girls who had taunted her about her accent and her thick glasses and her buck teeth.

Ugly girl. Yank. Weirdo-girl. Fleabag.

And now, here in the darkness, she had found a friend. A little glowing friend. A sphere, pulsing softly, like a plastic football lit from within. Lizzie had touched it. And in her head she had heard the voice.

What is your name, child?

Elizabeth Sarah Devonshire.

What is this place, child? What is the name of this world?

The world. It's called the world. I mean… Earth.

Earth! That is most appropriate.

And the voice had echoed deep in the caverns of her mind, and had told her what to do.

Every month, Lizzie Devonshire had returned to check on the sphere. It had helped her, guided her. Her entire life had been dedicated to the Consciousness from that moment on. Her business experience, her meeting with Sir Gerry, her involvement with Carson Polymers.

And every month, the sphere had grown.

Deep underground.

And, after ten years, the sprawling palace of fun had begun to grow above it. First called Superville, then Superland, and finally Hyperville, it had taken shape on the concrete foundations as a strong thermoplastic frame, stronger than iron and more flexible, a huge plastic spider squatting on the cold earth. And the Consciousness had drawn strength from the infrastructure, and from every shop and café and shop-window dummy and Zone and exhibit which was developed.

And now it reached out through Hyperville.

Miss Devonshire screamed as the Nestene Consciousness coursed through her.

TWELVE

'**W**hat was that?' said Chantelle.

Kate whirled round, doing a full circle, scanning the bar. 'I didn't hear anything.'

'It was—'

Chantelle didn't even get to finish her sentence. There was a loud thump, and the surface of the bar flipped open, taps and all – and a hand emerged, followed by an arm. And then a tousled quiff of hair and a big grin.

'All right, you lot!' said the Doctor briskly, hopping out into the saloon area and slamming the bar shut. 'Have you missed me?'

Sir Gerry gulped the rest of his whisky and slammed the empty glass down on the saloon bar. 'Dammit, Doctor, you seem to come and go as you please in Hyperville!'

'Well…' The Doctor shrugged. 'These maintenance hatches are all labelled. Just think of me as a sort of mystery shopper… Reece! Reecey Reece Reece, my man. Not feeling nauseous?'

'Not bad, Doctor.' Reece grinned weakly.

'Good.' The Doctor clapped Reece with both hands on his shoulders, then his cheeks, in a manner which Kate, grinning, recognised as belonging to an old comedian her mum had liked called Eric Morecambe. 'And Chantelle! Both OK? Good… Your mum's fine, by the way. Got people looking after her.'

'And Derek?' asked Chantelle.

The Doctor paused, his face giving everything away. 'I'm sorry,' he said. He put a hand on Chantelle's shoulder. 'We'll make sure he didn't die in vain.'

She shrugged. 'I never really liked him much.' She caught Reece's shocked gaze. 'Well, I didn't!' Embarrassed, she backtracked a little. 'But… he made Mum happy. So I'm sorry.'

The Doctor looked around the dimly lit saloon and his eyes alighted on Shaneeqi, who was standing, arms folded, outside on the terrace. Her eyes were still shaded with sunglasses, and she was staring out at the street. 'She all right?' he said quietly.

'Bit of a shock, I think,' said Kate quietly. 'It's not every day you have to admit your husband's actually an unfeeling killer plastic robot. Although, to be fair, my friend Melissa did say something similar when the Child Support Agency couldn't track hers down.'

'Kate Maguire!' said the Doctor. 'I like a woman who keeps her sense of humour in a time of crisis… Now then…' He rummaged in his capacious jacket pockets and pulled out a small jar. His face lit up with boyish delight as he held it up to the light. 'This might be just what we need. The whole tooth and nothing but the tooth. *Ohhhhyesss.*'

'That's from the Doomcastle!' said Chantelle, recognising it. 'You took it from that vampire bloke.'

'And if I'm right,' said the Doctor, 'and I often am – then this little incisor is going to help us out quite a bit.' He looked around. 'If Maxie-boy hadn't impounded my TARDIS, I could take this and analyse it properly.'

'What do you need, Doctor?' Kate asked.

'Well, I'm trying to formulate a bit of an anti-plastic cocktail.'

'*Anti*-plastic?'

'Anti-plastic! Interacts with the molecular structure of Plastinol-2. Causes it to disintegrate. Ideally, various combinations of chlorofluorocarbons, vinyl acetates? And copolymers with a dash of maleic anhydride?'

'Here!' Chantelle tossed him something and he caught it instinctively – her large can of hairspray.

The Doctor beamed in delight. 'Brilliant! Now all I need is some nitrocellulose and an adhesive polymer. A nice tosylamide-formaldehyde resin would do.'

Chantelle rummaged in her bag again, and pulled out her nail varnish. 'You're not gonna believe this, but this is patent Auton-dissolver.'

'You should have seen!' Reece punched the air. 'It was sick!'

'Sick?' The Doctor wrinkled his nose.

'That means good,' whispered Kate.

'Ah.' The Doctor reached out for the nail polish and held it up to the light. 'Seriously – you *attacked* the Autons with this?'

Chantelle nodded. 'Turned their plastic heads to soup.'

'How did you know it would work?'

Chantelle grinned. 'I didn't.'

The Doctor pulled a grudgingly admiring face. 'Empirical method. I like it. Much how I work myself. OK… Plastinol-2's still at an underdeveloped stage. If we're lucky, the Nestenes have overreached themselves this time… Now – somehow, I need to get hold of some kind of ethyl alcohol.'

'Ethyl alcohol?' said Kate. 'You mean booze?'

'Well…' The Doctor shrugged. 'If you like.'

Everybody looked at him.

Kate folded her arms and nodded over his left shoulder. The Doctor whirled round, then back to face Kate again. 'What?' he said.

'We're in a bar,' she said long-sufferingly.

The Doctor looked over his shoulder again, then back at Kate. 'What?'

'We – are – in – a – *bar*.'

The Doctor's face broke into a broad grin. 'Course we are! Brilliant!' He ran to the bar, vaulted over it and grabbed a pint glass. He pressed it against each of the optics in turn until the glass was brimming full of a brownish, unpleasant-looking mixture of spirits. 'Club Hyperville, the drinks are free!' He held it up to the light, dipped a finger in and tasted it. 'Mmmm. Wouldn't serve this up at Happy Hour, but it's just what we need… Gimme five minutes.'

'Doctor?' said Sir Gerry, his voice slightly lower than usual.

'Yes, Sir Gerry? What can I do for you? Don't tell me – bit of blue-skies thinking? Reference for Kate?' The Doctor stirred the mixture of drinks in the glass and started squirting hairspray into it. 'She's brilliant. *Brilliant*. Employ her. Let her run the place.'

'Well, I—'

'She'll give you a hundred per cent. Remember that – a *hundred* per cent. You can't have more than a hundred per cent. Anybody who says they're giving you more, check their CV and make sure they've got GCSE Maths. It's pretty easy. I think even I took that at some point, and I'm *rubbish* at exams... What was I saying? Yes! Kate! Brilliant!'

Sir Gerry sighed, his florid face creasing into a frown. 'I was actually going to ask,' he said patiently, 'if you knew what had happened to that daft pillock Max Carson.'

The Doctor's face clouded and he stared out at the terrace, looking past Shaneeqi into the sun-blasted desert beyond One Horse Town.

'Max is dead,' he said.

'How?' asked Sir Gerry, shocked.

The Doctor thought back. Max Carson's face screwed up with anger at the thought that he might lose his nest egg and his flat and his car... pumping bullets into Kendrick's Plastinol form... screaming in the corona of red light as his molecules were dispersed by the deadly Auton weaponry.

'Honourably,' said the Doctor softly. Then he nodded out into the street. 'Kate – keep watch for me.'

Shaneeqi, in the middle of the deserted street of One Horse Town, could not quite believe that she was still in Hyperville.

The sunshine felt real, as real as the sun of Florida and Majorca and Ibiza had felt. She cocked her head as if she had heard something. Majorca. Had she ever been to Majorca? She must have, but she couldn't remember when. Yes, she had stayed in the Hotel del Mar… No, the Hotel Hispania… Where *had* she stayed? And who with? And promoting which single?

Something very odd was happening. Shaneeqi suddenly found herself unable to remember any words of Spanish, and yet she *knew* she had learned the basics at least. She remembered leaning on the bar and chatting to Pedro the barman, and… Or was that something she had imagined? Something which had happened in a dream?

There was a sound. A door flapping and banging in the breeze.

Shaneeqi instantly crouched like a huntress, not quite knowing why. She had lowered her eyes in the direction of the sound, which seemed to have emanated from the bank.

She slowly walked down the dusty street towards it. One pace, two, three. For some bizarre reason she thought she had forgotten how to walk.

'Hey Baby, You're A Waste of Space.' That was it. That was the record she had been promoting in Majorca. Number 14 in the Spanish charts, just scraped the Top 40 in the UK. Well, it was the fourth single from the album. Relief coursed through her as she remembered.

But there was still something *wrong* with the memory.

Despite the sunlight, her arms and legs felt cold.

She whirled round.

She had been walking in the wrong direction. She was no longer alone in One Horse Town.

Two figures stood there, shadows long in the sunlight, faces almost entirely hidden in the shadow of their broad-brimmed cowboy hats. They wore denim shirts and battered canvas trousers. Both stood in the same pose, right hands hovering near their holstered guns.

Shaneeqi narrowed her eyes behind her shades.

She felt a tingle in her body. Not fear... something... *deeper...*

The cowboys both stepped forward, and as the sunlight fell on their faces she saw the lumpy, unfinished shapes of their heads.

Their eyes glowed an intense red, and as she took an involuntary step back, both cowboys went for their guns at the same time.

Paul Kendrick stood on the travelator and let it carry him down silently into the wreckage of Europa Plaza. Fragments of the vast and smooth window of the Megastore lay scattered across the floor, and the fronts of shops were burning with hot, orange intensity.

Kendrick stood in front of one of the burning shops.

He held his palms up, feeling the heat.

It had been a shoe shop, an exclusive boutique. He remembered going there, talking to the assistant, being measured for a stylish pair of boots. Was that a real memory, or one the Consciousness had given him?

He walked slowly along the mall. The artificial trees towered above him. He touched them, feeling the roughness of the bark. Just like real trees. Maybe oak, or beech. Just like in his garden.

Which garden? Where? Had he ever had a garden?

The trees were plastic, of course.

Plastic.

He reached out and touched the trunk again, and felt strengthened by its presence. He smiled.

There was one shop window still intact, the glass tinted dark blue so that it worked as an effective mirror.

He put his hands up to the glass and stared at himself. The same face, blue eyes, spiky hair, wide mouth which he had known for the past thirty years.

I am Paul Kendrick.

He tried to say it. Over and over again.

It just didn't sound right.

We are the Nestene Consciousness.

That sounded better.

How long did flesh last? Seventy, eighty years if you were lucky? And people… they were so badly designed. There was no structure to them. No precision. The most vulnerable organ, the brain – a squashy mass of cells – was placed on top of the body in a fragile container.

Why am I thinking like this?

This is madness!

I am Paul Kendrick! Paul Goldenball Kendrick!

I have heard the crowd chanting my name!

He pressed himself up close to the glass, so that he could see his stubble and the hints of crow's feet around his eyes. Shan liked them, he remembered. She called it mature-looking.

He stroked the thin, sandpaper-rough layer of stubble on his face. When had he started shaving? Thirteen, fourteen? Granddad Kendrick had bought him his first electric razor, for his birthday. It had been wrapped in gold paper. Tied with a silver ribbon.

Where had that come from? It felt like a new memory. As if it had crashed into his mind, fired there like a goal out of nowhere.

Do not dwell on these things.

We are the Nestene Consciousness.

Think with us, join with us, be us.

Kendrick smiled.

'We are the Nestene Consciousness,' he said softly.

He nodded to himself, and enjoyed seeing the soft pink glow in his eyes, hazed into purple by the tinted blue of the shopfront.

It all made sense again, now.

He became aware that he was not alone.

He spun around.

The wobbling, chuckling form of Beta-4 stood there behind him. The glossy, black-plastic Auton dummy, its face fixed in a rictus grin, little hands clenching and unclenching.

'I know, Beta-4,' he said softly. 'You want to play.'

He turned away from the shopfront and marched forward into the shattered mall.

All organics within the perimeter zone must be eliminated.

'Let's finish it off,' he said coldly.

The Doctor was shaking the ingredients furiously in a cocktail-shaker. The mixture smelt vile, Kate thought – like paint-stripper mixed with a drunk's breath.

'Haha!' The Doctor seemed to be relishing the challenge, as usual. 'A one, a two, a one-two-three-four! Not exactly going to be a Harvey Wallbanger, this.'

'More of an Auton Headbanger,' suggested Kate.

The Doctor grinned. 'I like that!' He poured a little of the liquid into a small tequila glass. It was pink and frothing, and reminded Kate of the stuff you had to rinse and spit with at the dentist's surgery. He held the plastic vampire tooth up above the glass. 'Now, watch this.'

He let go of the tooth. Kate saw it plop into the foul liquid, and for a second it frothed and fizzed like an aspirin. Then it dissolved, as if it had never existed. There was a vinegary, plasticky smell, which was gone in a second.

'Anti-plastic, fantastic,' said the Doctor softly. 'Even better than my last formulation, if I do say so myself.'

'And that's our secret weapon?'

'Well, one of them.' The Doctor grinned at Kate. 'You're the other.'

'Me?'

'Well, you and Reece and Chantelle. I'll explain what I need from you.'

'And this… Consciousness – it affiliates itself with *all* plastic?' Kate thought she had grasped the concept, but wanted to be sure of the details.

The Doctor nodded. 'Its molecular structure is tuned into it.' He added another dash of whisky to his shaker. 'It's a natural home for the gestalt entity to spread its tentacles into.'

'But it's contained within Hyperville?'

'For now. I imagine we're a sort of testing ground. When the Nestene cluster reaches an appropriate point in your solar system, it'll energise the Consciousness and link to the warp-shunt output. Give it a burst, a boost, a…' The Doctor flung his arms out wide, making Kate duck. 'A massive influx of *power*. And then, I imagine, the Central Program will activate something else… What, I'm not sure y—'

He was interrupted as the explosive, terrifying sound of gunshots echoed through the street. The Doctor looked up in alarm. Kate ran for the door, and Sir Gerry was there with her.

'Be careful!' the Doctor shouted.

Kate ran out onto the terrace, and for a second she could not understand what had happened. Shaneeqi was facing the two gunslingers dead-on, their pistols smoking, and yet she appeared unharmed.

'Shaneeqi!' Kate yelled. 'Get back in here!'

'It's OK, lass,' Sir Gerry began.

The girl looked over at Kate, confused, and then made a run for it, diving as the sharpshooters fired again.

Kate, Shaneeqi and Sir Gerry ducked behind the tables in front of the saloon, bullets zinging into the woodwork all around and exploding in puffs of smoke.

'It's OK,' Shaneeqi said, having got her breath back. 'They're not real. The bullets.'

'What?' Kate was confused.

Shaneeqi grabbed Kate's arms and looked at her. 'Kate. I know now. I understand. My life is—'

'They're the Sharpshooter Twins!' Sir Gerry's delighted exclamation cut off whatever Shaneeqi had been going to say. 'We put the tourists up against 'em. They love it.' His face fell. 'Usually,' he added.

On the other side of the street, the door of the bank smashed open, shattering to splinters as a phalanx of Auton mannequins broke through.

Shaneeqi, Kate and Sir Gerry gawped in horror. Behind them, the Doctor peered at the dummies through his glasses, checking readings on his liminal energy detector.

'Doctor!' Kate said, with a rising warning tone in her voice.

'I know, I *know*!'

Looking incongruous in the Wild West setting, the

dummies strode into the street and began to fan out, covering every entrance and exit. With a shiver, Kate noted that their gait was stronger and more powerful now – they had none of the lolloping drunkenness of before.

Behind them came the toy dolls, chattering and waddling like grotesque mini-parodies of children, some with their little heads swivelling full circle on their necks, little hands reaching out for a deadly hug.

'Oh, no,' Kate muttered.

'After today,' Sir Gerry growled, 'no more bloody shop-window dummies. I'm never having them in any shop, ever again!'

Miss Devonshire's scream seemed to grow deeper, slower, to undulate.

And a millisecond later, the pod shattered, infused with greenish light and vapour, breaking into a shower of tiny fragments which broke into tinier fragments, scattering themselves over Miss Devonshire, swirling around her like a tornado of plastiglass, enveloping her.

Miss Devonshire's body, like a green ghost, warped and rippled and fused with the seething tentacles of the Consciousness's physical form.

'Are you OK?' Kate asked Shaneeqi.

'Yes,' she said, sounding distant. 'I'm fine.'

'Look!' Chantelle said. 'Look at Bruce Wayne and his mate.'

The Sharpshooter Twins were oscillating wildly, as if unsure about the new arrivals.

But now the Autons, too, stood still in the sunlit street and, as one, their hands went to their heads – as if they were in pain, or maybe as if they were preparing to listen intently to new instructions.

'Fascinating,' the Doctor murmured. 'Auton confusion. Just confirms my theory.'

Kate looked at him. 'It does?'

'It won't last long, though. Come on. I'm going to get us one.'

'You're *what*?'

'Hold that.' The Doctor gave her the cocktail shaker full of anti-plastic and, ducking, dodged out into the street, heading for the Sharpshooter Twins.

'He's mad,' Chantelle murmured.

'Yup,' said Kate. 'By the way – Bruce Wayne is Batman. You mean John Wayne.'

'Oh, *whatever*. Who are you, my mum?'

Kate wasn't listening. 'I've got to help him,' she said. 'Hold this.' Kate shoved the cocktail-shaker at Shaneeqi and followed the Doctor.

The Doctor had ducked round behind one of the Sharpshooter Twins, and was trying to find the right spot to activate his sonic screwdriver on its neck. He did a double take when he saw her. 'Kate, get back!'

Kate grabbed the Auton's gun-arm and tried to push it upwards. She was amazed at the strength in it, the sheer power pushing against her like angry machinery within the rippling plastic. There was something else, too, thought Kate – the ground itself seemed to be vibrating beneath her feet.

'Now, Doctor!' she yelled. 'Do it now!'

A blue glow fizzed around the Auton's head, and it slumped. The Doctor caught it under the arms.

'There,' the Doctor said. 'Just what we need. What shall we call this feller? How about Joe? Joe Auton. That'll do.' He shoved the sonic screwdriver into the Auton's ear, making delicate adjustments.

The other Autons began, slowly and stiffly, to move their plastic limbs again.

'Doctor!' Kate said urgently.

'I know!' He reached out his hand, still supporting the Sharpshooter under the shoulder with the other. 'Is your phone internet-linked?'

Kate looked puzzled. 'Aren't they all?' she asked.

The Doctor didn't pursue this. He thumbed several buttons at lightning speed, and the phone beeped as he sent a message. 'Nasty migraine! Got it again!'

The Autons froze like statues.

The Doctor threw Kate's phone back to her and nodded. 'Each time it'll take them less time to unscramble it. Won't hold for long. Get the others.'

'Where are we going?'

He looked up at Kate. 'To the station. Get everyone on to the train!'

The giant glistening eye, blazing with intelligence, bubbled and warped and inflated like a balloon.

Elizabeth Devonshire, arms thrust upwards, screeched as she achieved the zenith of her life.

And then her outstretched fingers, greenish-pink in hue, began to grow, and grow, and grow, thrashing like tentacles, wrapping themselves around the pillars and girders of the underground warehouse.

Hyperville shook.

Hyperville *throbbed*.

And Miss Devonshire ascended.

'All aboard!' called the Doctor. 'Right then! Under bridges, over bridges, et cetera, et cetera!'

With the Doctor at the controls, the little train began to chug its way across the fake desert landscape, heading for an illusory horizon. As it clanked and chugged along the metal rails, they passed through convincing rocks and cacti, and Kate was sure she saw a shape crouched behind one of them.

'Get down!' she shouted.

The white-hatted cowboy who had popped up like a jack-in-the box from behind the rocks fired his pistol. Chantelle screamed, clutching Kate and Reece. A second later, they were soaked with water.

'Just a bit of fun,' said Sir Gerry from behind them in the carriage. 'Kiddies love it, y'know.' He shook his head. 'At least, they did.'

Reece looked behind, to where the blank-faced Sharpshooter, seemingly inert but with its pistol levelled, sat propped between Sir Gerry and Shaneeqi.

'Why did we have to bring old Joe with us?' he said nervously. 'He gives me the creeps.'

'Doctor's idea,' said Sir Gerry briskly, as the train swerved round a corner and entered a tunnel in the rocks. 'Chap seems to know what he's doing. Best leave him to it.'

Kate had climbed to the front of the train and was peering over the Doctor's shoulder. 'You said you had something for me to do?'

'Hyperville has a deluge sprinkler-system. I want you to locate the main pipe source, and release the anti-plastic cocktail into the system at the top of the Administration building. Thirtieth floor.' He grinned. 'I memorised the maintenance plan earlier.'

'OK... Will there be enough?'

'Once the anti-plastic attaches itself to the polar molecules in the water, it'll adhere and replicate. It should spread through the system in a matter of seconds.' The Doctor pulled a face. 'Well, that's the theory. Whooh!' He sounded the hooter on the train. 'You know, I've *always* wanted to drive one of these.'

'Uh-huh. Doctor. Stick to the point.'

'The sprinkler network's activated in Zones by fire-hazard signals. If I can get them all to activate together, the Autons will get a shock.'

'So why do you need to go and talk to them?'

The Doctor's expression hardened. 'Because I want to give Miss Devonshire the choice.'

Kate thought for a moment, and found her hand closing over the Hypercard in her pocket. She held it out to the Doctor. 'You'll need this,' she said.

'What?' He looked confused.

'I don't know why. I just know that you need it.'

'Who told you?'

Kate smiled. 'You did,' she said. 'Four years ago. When I first met you.'

THIRTEEN

Carmine light drenched the malls. Long shadows stretched over the wall and floor. The hot, sticky smell of plastic was everywhere.

They filled the aisles. The silent shop-window dummies. The chattering, chuckling dolls, scurrying around their feet like eager pink puppies.

In Europa Plaza, or what remained of it, the central, glass lift shaft lay in pieces on the marble floor. Green light streamed from it, and the new, renewed physical form of the Nestene Consciousness stepped forth.

It was a form that bore a resemblance to a human female – to Elizabeth Devonshire, no less. Her brown hair, now loose, streamed out behind her as if in a strong wind, and her eyes, now devoid of their spectacles, glowed with an intense green, the same greenish hue which suffused her glistening skin. Her suit had transformed itself into reddish-gold, shiny like a fleshy, living plastic, merging with her arms and legs. She stepped forward, booted feet making a soft, slurping, squelching noise on the floor, as if the boots themselves were alive. And she smiled, the same broad, tight clownish smile with which Miss Devonshire had charmed her adversaries and her associates alike – but there was something cold about it now. Something plastic.

She spread her arms out wide, and her fingers snaked, grew, expanded, uncoiling themselves like greenish-pink tendrils, coiling up towards the vaulted roof and the higher levels and the Oculators, punching holes in the fabric of Hyperville and fusing with its being.

After a moment, Paul Kendrick stepped forward from the crowd of Autons. He tilted his head to one side as he surveyed the human face before him.

'What are you?' he said.

We are the Nestene Consciousness. We have new form.

'But I sense… another.'

The human woman, Miss Devonshire, has given herself up to us. She has been with us for thirty years. She has always been with us, and now she is one of us.

Miss Devonshire's green eyes flicked upwards.

'Behold the final movement in our symphony,' she said.

Sir Gerry Hobbes-Mayhew was not having a good day.

He liked to think of himself as a successful man. Tough but fair, respected in his industry. After a chain of sports clubs and a media empire, Hyperville had been his big project, his dream – somewhere to entertain the entire family under one roof.

Somewhere for an hour, a morning, a day, even a week's

holiday. People had laughed when he suggested the latter, and yet the pair of four-star hotels in the complex always found themselves with healthy bookings.

They'd suffered a bit in the global recession, but nothing like as much as people had said they would. Hyperville had gone from strength to strength. And it seemed – with Miss Devonshire and Max Carson on board and the new Plastinol-2 range scaled out through the complex, so incredibly cheap and amazingly versatile – that nothing could go wrong. Nothing at all.

He'd never expected to find himself clinging on for dear life to the Hyperville Train, behind a grinning, wild-haired madman in a brown suit, accompanied by one of the Sharpshooter Twins from Wild West World, as the train swerved and juddered through the tunnels on its way to goodness only knew where.

'Where are we *going*, Doctor?' Sir Gerry shouted, as the tunnels hurtled past. He was starting to wish he had consulted the interactive Hyperville plans a little more closely.

Buffeted by the airflow, the Doctor consulted the compass-like device in his hand. 'Level Zero!' he yelled. 'But maybe not by the quickest route!'

The train lurched, heading round a sharp corner towards what looked like a dead end.

'Doctor!' Sir Gerry's stomach plummeted and he couldn't bear to look. 'The doors!'

'What?'

'The doors, you daft pillock!'

'Oh! Yes, right!' The Doctor activated his sonic screwdriver just in time, and what looked like a dark, solid brick wall in front of them blossomed open, allowing the train to hurtle forwards into the glass-covered Atrium. Like the rest of Hyperville, the Atrium was bathed in the ruddy glow of the emergency lighting – which made it seem a sinister, shadowy place, and not the welcoming, bright space of before.

The train burst out into the vast space.

And slowed.

Sir Gerry looked upwards into the vast glass dome.

It was flecked with black shapes, he saw. Bats? No… He suddenly realised what they were, and it chilled his blood.

Green, cackling faces set rigidly, cloaks streaming out behind them, gnarled plastic hands gripping plastic broomsticks, the witches circled and swooped.

The Doctor jerked the train to a standstill and scrambled back through the carriages. He adjusted a setting on his sonic screwdriver. 'Time for Joe to come to our rescue…' he murmured.

And at that instant, the Sharpshooter sat bolt upright, and jammed his pistol into Sir Gerry's back.

Kate stared up into the gaping, dark concrete lift shaft. She made sure the backpack was firmly attached to her and turned to Chantelle.

'Right. Plan B.'

Chantelle and Reece held up their containers of hairspray and nodded.

'Can't you just take the stairs?' Reece asked, staring in dismay into the emptiness of the shaft.

'You heard what the Doctor said,' Kate murmured grimly. 'The Autons will have the stairs covered. And with the lifts deactivated, there's not much choice if we want to get to the highest point of the water system.' She nodded to Chantelle.

'Your phone's with the Doctor?'

Chantelle nodded.

'As soon as I send the signal,' Kate reminded her, 'the sprinkler-system will kick in. That's if the Doctor's jiggery-pokery has all worked right.' She pulled a face. 'Let's hope it has.'

'I'll come with you,' said Shaneeqi.

Kate looked doubtful. 'The Doctor told me to do this bit alone. It needs three of you to guard the access-ways, make sure the Autons don't get up here.'

'I'm coming with you,' said Shaneeqi, sounding resolute. And she swung herself into the darkness, hand over hand, slim body rippling under her tight T-shirt and leather trousers. She glared down at Kate. 'Well?'

Kate sighed. She swung herself into the lift shaft. It was cold, eerie and smelled of metal and oil. 'Whatever happens,' she said to Reece and Chantelle, 'hold them back.'

The teenagers nodded.

'Wait!'

The Doctor stood up as the train slowed. He held his hand up to the witches, like a policeman trying to stop traffic. Sir Gerry looked worriedly from the Doctor to the Autons, worrying that he had gone too far again.

The phalanx of witches hovered above the train, eyes glowing.

'Gas-jet levitation,' said the Doctor to Sir Gerry. 'One of Miss Devonshire's little tricks, I believe?'

Sir Gerry looked shamefaced. 'I deal with facts and figures, Doctor. I'm a plain feller. Not that much into the newfangled stuff. Afraid I've always tended to leave the technical gizmos to Miss Devonshire and Carson.' He shuddered. 'Poor Max.'

As one, their heads turned to face the Doctor and their eyes glowed green.

'We come as prisoners,' said the Doctor. 'Look.' And he nodded to the Sharpshooter.

The cowboy, the one which the Doctor had referred to as Joe Auton and which had been inert for the entire journey, was now sitting bolt upright, pointing its gun at them. Its waxy, pale face held the hint of a sneer.

There was a crackle, as if the witches were receiving instructions in the ether.

The Doctor gave Sir Gerry a quick wink.

'OK, then?' he said with a nonchalant smile.

The witches spoke as one. 'You will come with us.'

'Oh, yes. Absolutely. We're right there.' The Doctor grinned. 'Wouldn't want to let you ladies down.'

Kate was beginning to wonder how on Earth she'd got into this.

'I'm telling you,' she gasped down to Shaneeqi, as she hauled herself up the metal maintenance ladder, hand-over-hand, 'if Sir Gerry doesn't give me a job after this, he never will. I mean, I know I came here to expose the secrets of Hyperville, but I think that one's pretty much out in the open.' She paused for a rest. 'You OK down there, Shaneeqi?'

'Fine.' The girl's voice was dull, emotionless.

Kate caught her breath. 'You know, Shan… Can I call you Shan? I feel like I know you. I've bought all your downloads, after all. It must be great just to… know what you're going to do in life and just… *do* it. Don't you think?'

'Uh-huh.'

'I mean… the Doctor, look at him. I don't know who he is, where he comes from. I don't think he's even… well, I don't think he's even *human*. But he seems to know his purpose in life. Seems to know the point of it all.' She glanced down. 'Am I getting too philosophical for you, Shan?'

Shaneeqi smiled weakly. 'Possibly.'

'Sorry.'

'Did you… you know, always want to do… what you do?'

She frowned. 'I can't remember.'

'What do you mean?' asked Kate.

'I mean I can't remember.' She looked up at Kate with panic in her eyes.

'But you started out singing in clubs, right? Then you were discovered. I was reading about it on your website.'

'It's all invented,' Shaneeqi said softly.

Kate grinned. 'Marketing hype, yeah? Oh, well.' She began to haul herself up the ladder again. 'Come on. Let's do this.'

Deep down in the lift shaft, there was a clunk and a whirr. It reverberated through the entire shaft, and Kate felt it in her hands. Feeling as if her stomach had turned to liquid, she tried to turn round and look. 'What was that?'

Shaneeqi was looking down into the shaft. Slowly, she turned her face upwards to look at Kate.

'The lift,' she said. 'It's coming.'

There was another clunk from the shaft above them. Like the sound of some great animal in pain, the gears screamed, and then Kate could see the cables beginning to move.

For a moment she panicked. Then she told herself it was pointless, that she had to do something. She had to focus.

'Climb,' she snapped to Shaneeqi. 'We've got to climb!'

***

Accompanied by the witches, the Doctor and Sir Gerry ascended the escalator to the shattered ruins of Europa Plaza. Behind them, the Sharpshooter kept his pistol trained on them.

Inside the Doctor's pocket was Chantelle's mobile phone, set to vibrate. He was waiting for a signal from Kate.

Long shadows fell across the Plaza. Autons. Hundreds of them, all lined up and ready, eyes gently glowing pinkish-red. And the dolls, more jittery but still ready.

'Playtime!' said the Doctor cheerfully.

'*Doctor*,' said the reverberating, gurgling voice which was part Elizabeth Devonshire, part alien. '*How pleasant to see you again.*'

'Miss Devonshire. If I can call you that. Is that your real name?' The Doctor became aware of the silence that had fallen. 'Sorry. I expect you want to speak.'

She took a deep, juddering breath. '*The Hyperville experiment has been a success,*' she said. '*In precisely seven minutes, the Cluster will be within transmission range of Earth.*'

'Ah. Right.' The Doctor tried to look nonchalant.

'The Cluster?' Sir Gerry looked worried.

'Shower of meteorites. Well, that's what it'll look like. If Jodrell Bank are interested at all. Doubt anybody will shoot them down.'

'And what are they really?' Sir Gerry asked nervously.

'A Nestene swarm. Spherical pods. Seeds, if you like. Each ready to bounce its signal off the Consciousness, and tune into the plastic-based environments like this around the world. Am I right, Miss Devonshire?'

'*You are correct, Doctor.*'

'In about…' The Doctor checked his watch. 'Six minutes?'

Miss Devonshire smiled. '*Correct, Doctor.*'

The Doctor stepped forward. 'There's still time to stop.'

'*The Nestene Consciousness does not stop.*'

'Listen to me. *You*, Miss Devonshire. Because, you know what? There is a little corner of the Nestene Consciousness which is forever Elizabeth Devonshire. I can hear it. I'm asking you not to do this.'

'*There is no choice, Doctor. It is done.*'

The Doctor took a step backwards. He looked into the bright green eyes of the Consciousness, as if weighing up the truth of the words.

'Then I'm sorry,' said the Doctor. 'I really am.' He glanced at Sir Gerry. 'Now!' he yelled.

The Doctor and Sir Gerry dropped to the ground.

The Sharpshooter raised its pistol in both hands.

And fired.

The lift was thundering upwards, the rumbling getting louder and louder. Kate knew they were not going to make it. Hand over hand, she climbed as if trapped in some terrible dream.

The lift growled on upwards. Kate could see the forbidding, black square of its roof, cutting out the light below.

'Hang on!' Shaneeqi said. She looked across the shaft at Kate. 'Jump!'

Kate knew it would buy them vital seconds. She and Shaneeqi stared at each other across the shaft, and Kate nodded, and then, in unison, they sprang from the ladder and landed like cats on the juddering roof of the lift. Pain crashed through Kate's knee, but she winced and tried to ignore it.

Kate looked up.

The top of the shaft was getting closer and closer. She

estimated that they had maybe thirty seconds before the lift reached the top and crushed them. It was not going to be a pleasant way to die.

'That didn't do us much good,' she said softly to Shaneeqi.

Kate glanced up. The young star was standing, stretching herself up to her full height.

'What are you *doing*?' Kate gasped.

'What I was made for,' Shaneeqi answered.

And when Kate looked into her eyes, she saw the faintest hint of a pinkish glow.

'Oh, no,' she breathed.

The flicker of a smile spread across Shaneeqi's face.

'I want to say I'm sorry,' she said. 'But I can't.'

FOURTEEN

The Sharpshooter fired at Miss Devonshire – not the fake bullets from the Wild West World, but a sizzling bolt of blood-red Nestene energy.

Miss Devonshire's hand came up, moving as fast as an expert tennis player. The beam bounced off, reflecting back at the Sharpshooter, and impacting with its head. Its cowboy hat was blown off in smoking tatters, and the top of its head smashed like an eggshell, the fragments scattering across the Plaza, popping and fizzing.

The Doctor and Sir Gerry slowly lifted their heads, looking at the gashed shell of the Sharpshooter's head, which was belching noxious black smoke like a miniature volcano.

'*Any further tricks, Doctor?*' asked Miss Devonshire. '*I thought not. Hold them.*'

Two of the Auton catering-staff stepped forward, grabbing the Doctor and Sir Gerry and pinning their arms behind their backs. Beside Miss Devonshire, Beta-4 jumped up and down, chuckling and gurgling.

'*Four minutes,*' said Miss Devonshire.

High above the planet, the group of pulsing spheres began to move a little wider apart. Their glow became a deeper purple, more intense.

They hovered above the cratered surface of Earth's moon, facing the beautiful blue planet on the horizon.

The Cluster was ready.

In the Plaza, the Doctor pulled a puzzled face. 'How are you going to do it, exactly? I mean, your previous attempts at invasion didn't go brilliantly, did they?'

'*The last attempts were strong but not strategic. This one is coordinated.*'

'Humans are *good*, you know. They make stuff. They're resourceful. They know what they're doing.' The Doctor nodded at Sir Gerry. 'Take this chap, for example. Sir Gerry Hobbes-Mayhew. Plain old Gerry Mayhew when he was at school. Decent pupil, nothing outstanding. But now he owns businesses worth millions. Creates jobs for thousands of people in depressed areas. Gives loads to charity and doesn't shout about it.'

Sir Gerry looked nervous.

'All on Wikipedia, Sir Gerry,' whispered the Doctor.

'*Humans are imperfect. They are flawed.*'

'Ohhhh, yes! They're flawed! That's the *beauty* of them.' The Doctor looked defiant. 'Last time, they defended themselves. Some of them did pretty well. So what are you doing? How are you going to subjugate an entire population?'

Miss Devonshire laughed. *'You have the evidence in your pocket, Doctor.'*

The Doctor frowned. 'Really?'

'Each and every shopper here – and there are millions of them – has a Hypercard. The Hypercard is made of Plastinol-2. It is designed to attach itself to the cells of the human skin – leaving an imperceptible trace. When the signal comes, Doctor, the Plastinol cells will grow, increase, multiply. The Plastinol will spread across each human being who has shopped here. Just like that poor journalist. Oh, but you never saw her! It was truly beautiful.'

'Horrible,' said the Doctor coldly.

'You may think so, Doctor. But you are a fool.'

The Doctor pulled a face. 'You think *I'm* a fool? You're the one who fell for the old Wookie Prisoner Trick.'

Miss Devonshire's eyes blazed.

'Two minutes, Doctor.'

It seemed to be getting faster and louder as they reached the top. Kate could smell heat and oil and hot metal in her nostrils.

She was sure, crouched there on the juddering lift roof, that she was going to be sick.

And then Shaneeqi reached her right hand upwards, palm flat, and slammed it against the side of the lift shaft.

Gears ground. Metal screeched. The lift throbbed and vibrated. Kate could hear the mechanism screeching and grinding. She looked up in astonishment at the cables, which were holding steady. Shaneeqi lowered her eyes at Kate, and then Kate saw her left hand struggling to raise itself.

'I hear the voice of the Consciousness, Kate,' she said. 'I know. I've known for a while.'

'Shaneeqi…' Kate was painfully aware that she couldn't hold the lift for long.

'All of my life,' Shaneeqi said, 'before my career. All an invention. How do you think that feels?' Her voice was almost a whisper as she added, 'I wonder how many more of us there are out there.'

Her arm, flexed and rippling, was juddering.

Kate's eyes bulged in horror and she got up, pain crashing in her knee again, and hobbled to the edge of the lift's roof.

'I'm sorry,' said Shaneeqi again. 'So sorry.'

Her left arm came up, smartly, robotically.

There was a slurp and a crack, and her fingers split open as if gashed, revealing a horrible darkness within.

And then there was a mechanical *clunk*, and the slim tube of an Auton gun extended neatly from the blunt end of her wrist, pointing straight at Kate.

'Go,' said Shaneeqi, gritting her teeth. She nodded to the ladder. 'I can't hold it much longer.'

Kate did not know if she meant the lift, or something else.

She did not wait around to find out.

Ignoring the stabbing pain in her knee, Kate climbed and climbed, hauling herself up, sweating, desperate, knowing she only had three floors to climb.

Then two.

She risked a glance over her shoulder. Shaneeqi was still standing there, feet apart, arm braced against the shaft wall, holding the juddering, screaming lift in place.

Then one.

Sparks flashed in the shaft below. Kate knew she only had seconds. She hauled herself up the last few rungs of the maintenance ladder.

At the very top, there was a hatchway with a sturdy-looking wheel to turn. She grabbed it, pulled it. To her relief, it began to turn and the hatchway began to creak open.

And the lift started to rise.

Sparking, thundering, creaking, it ascended.

Kate hauled the hatchway open and hurled herself through with seconds to spare, rolling over into a dark, bare, tiled area.

The lift shrieked past, and there was a screeching, cracking noise, which Kate tried to block out.

Gasping and sweating, Kate stood up, surveying the area quickly. One wall was given over to a vast metal tank, which she knew to be one end of the water reserves. It was covered with a vast, snaking metal pipe, moulded in burnished red steel and about fifty centimetres in diameter. A confusing array of valves and pressure-gauges adorned the pipework.

'OK,' Kate murmured, pushing sweat-soaked hair out of her eyes. 'Here goes nothing.'

Kate pulled the cocktail-shaker from the rucksack. She knew all she had to do was to get the Doctor's anti-plastic formula into the system. Then, she just had to use her phone to send a signal pre-programmed by the Doctor and the sprinkler system would start up.

She scrambled towards the pipework on the walls. She unscrewed the nearest valve-wheel. It was stiff, and wouldn't move.

'Step aside.'

Kate looked up, her heart pounding.

It was Kendrick. He had emerged from the door to the stairs. His gun-arm was already extended, the tube pointing straight at her head.

Kate grinned. 'Goldenball Paul. Never thought it would come to this.'

'Step aside, or you will be destroyed.'

Kate did not remove her hands from the wheel. 'You must be kidding,' she said. 'I've come all this way. By the way – sorry about your missus. I think she's due the posthumous Greatest Hits collection.'

Kendrick's eyes glowed. The whine of the Auton energy built up.

Kate rolled to one side.

The beam flashed across the maintenance area, exploding against the huge pipe.

It burst.

It exploded in a thunderous jet of water, a vast gout spurting up and hitting the ceiling, drenching the room, steaming in the heat.

In the haze, Kate struggled to see Kendrick. But she skidded to the edge of the tank, undid the cocktail-shaker and hurled it deep into the pipe.

Kendrick advanced on her through the cascade of water.

Kate, pushing her wet hair aside, pulled out her phone and levelled it at him in both hands, like a weapon.

'I know what you're thinking,' she said with a grin. 'It's just a phone.'

Kendrick tilted his head on one side.

'But seeing as this is the Contakta 4500 with full 80-meg broadband and sat-link facility, the most powerful phone in the world, you've got to ask yourself one question – do I feel lucky?' Kate grinned and winked. 'Well, do you, mate?'

She pressed SEND.

***

In the Doctor's pocket, Chantelle's phone vibrated.

The Doctor's eyes opened wide as the blare of the alarms began to echo through Hyperville.

'Bad luck, then, Miss D,' he said. 'I think things are about to get a little damp.'

In every mall, in every shop, the nozzles of sprinklers descended from the ceilings.

They sprouted from the artificial sky in the WinterZone and the SherwoodZone and Wild West World, and popped from the cobwebbed chandeliers and vaulted ceilings of the Doomcastle. And a microsecond later, triggered by the phone signal, the deluge system kicked in with all the tremendous force its designers had given it.

Powerful jets shot from the nozzles. Gallons of water pounded from the ceiling like a monsoon, drenching and pounding Hyperville.

Water smacked the floor like the sound of a billion kisses.

Cold, clear water danced on the floors, sparkled and streamed off the shopfronts, filled the Plazas and the Atrium like a storm.

The Doctor, soaked immediately, could hardly see Sir Gerry in the haze. He struggled to get free from his Auton captors, but could still hardly move. Then he noticed the hands which held him were becoming looser.

He wriggled free.

The Auton was staggering, buckling under the impact of the pounding water.

The Doctor looked around. It was happening all over the Plaza – Autons' faces and heads beginning to dissolve like molten candles as the water, infused with anti-plastic molecules, streamed down on them.

The water sparkled and churned as it hit the marble floors of Hyperville, streaming down the escalators, pouring from the balconies into the Atrium. It had a powerful, pungent smell, like nail varnish mixed with wine.

'Kate did it,' he murmured.

Sir Gerry, soaked and bedraggled, was there beside the Doctor. 'How's it happening so *fast?*' he yelled above the thunderous noise of the water.

The Doctor wiped his eyes. 'Molecular adhesion!' he shouted. 'Anti-plastic bonds to the polar hydrocarbon molecules as soon as it comes into contact. Replicates the ethyl alcohol solution instantly!'

'I'll take your word for it,' Sir Gerry growled. 'You owe me for a new suit, you daft beggar!'

'I'll buy you a hundred!' The Doctor nodded. 'Right now, I think that's the least of our problems!'

Sir Gerry spun round. The Consciousness was there, water streaming off it, eyes blazing bright green, its finger-tendrils expanding into multiple tentacles, reaching out for every corner of Hyperville.

'*You will die!*'

The voice was now nothing like Miss Devonshire's. It was a deep, screeching howl, as if borne across the wastes of Time.

'*You will die for this!*'

Beta-4 staggered through the torrents, its little hands reaching out to clutch the Doctor and Sir Gerry. But before it reached them, its feet had begun to dissolve like sugar. As they watched, Beta-4's face began to bubble and stream with molten plastic like a waxwork exposed to a fire. In seconds, it was an unidentifiable blob of plastic, dwindling to a black puddle on the floor.

The Doctor took Chantelle's phone out again, and the Hypercard which Kate had given him. 'One more thing. I need to direct the frequency of the feedback loop. Maximise the signal.' He jammed the Hypercard into the slot at the back of the phone. '*Voilà.*'

'Doctor!' Sir Gerry had been grabbed by one of the pink tentacles, and was slowly being pulled into the heaving, green centre of the Consciousness, which now had only a roughly humanoid form. 'Do summat, ye cloth-head!'

'Just a couple more calibrations! *Oooff!*' The Doctor was pulled flat on his back on the soaking floor, and Chantelle's phone, with the Hypercard plugged into it, shot from his grasp, skittering across the soaked Plaza.

He grabbed for it, but it had gone – and now he, too, was being dragged by a grasping tentacle towards the Consciousness. It wrapped itself around his leg, tight as a plastic cord.

All around, the Autons sagged, sinking to their knees. The witches on their broomsticks crashed, hitting the great glass Waterwall and fracturing it, sending further cascades out into the Plaza. The small dolls had already dissolved into shapeless pink blobs.

The Doctor cast a helpless look at Sir Gerry. 'I didn't get to press Send! It won't work!'

Above the moon, the spheres of the Cluster pulsed.

Their purple light spread over the moondust and the craters, lighting up the dark sky. They hovered. They prepared to draw closer.

The time was almost at hand.

***

Down the soaking escalators came two figures, hazy in the steam of the Plaza.

'Chantelle! Reece!' The Doctor yelled. 'The phone! *Get the phone!*'

Chantelle looked around, uncertain at first as to where the Doctor was desperately trying to point.

Then she saw.

She scooped the phone up with both hands, dodging the flailing limbs of the Auton-waitress in front of her.

'Send!' the Doctor yelled. 'Send the signal!'

Chantelle was knocked flying by the thrashing Auton.

The phone flew from her hands, pirouetting through the air.

Reece cupped his hands like a fielder. And, seemingly to his own surprise, he caught it smartly. He stared at the phone in his hands in astonishment.

'Send, Reece! *Send!*' yelled the Doctor.

But something odd was happening to the phone.

It had curled up in Reece's hand like a giant slug. And now it extruded plastic tendrils from every corner, black slithering tentacles of plastic which wrapped themselves around his hand, tightening on it, cutting off the blood supply.

Reece yelped in horror and fell to his knees, hand held out, looking at the living-plastic phone in horror, feeling the clammy plastic tightening its grip.

At the edge of his mind, on the other side of the rushing streams of water, he heard the Doctor's voice.

'Just press the button, Reece! Do it!'

Reece reached out, eyes shut, and stabbed at the SEND button.

The final calibration pulsed through the systems of

the Central Program, hitting the nervous system of the Consciousness like a freight-train.

It screamed.

High above the Earth's moon, the cluster of spheres lost their purple glow. Each of them crunched and crumpled as if buckling under some internal gravity.

Then, as one, they dropped into the moondust and lay inert.

The Nestene Consciousness screamed and screamed, the sound echoing through every hall and mall and balcony. Carrying through the shattered ruins of Hyperville like a requiem.

The phone's tentacles curled up, as if it was a dying insect, and it unravelled itself from Reece, flopping inert and molten to the wet floor. Reece gaped in horror at the white weals on his hand.

The Consciousness thrashed, its protuberances letting go of the Doctor and Sir Gerry.

Its web of pinkish-green tendrils, reaching up and out and into every surface of Hyperville, rippled and throbbed as if a huge electrical charge had been pumped into it.

At its centre, the figure which had once been human, had once been Elizabeth Devonshire, bucked and thrashed. Its mouth opened wide and dark, pulling apart so wide that it seemed to rip, the face which had once been Elizabeth Devonshire's collapsing in on itself.

The tentacles began to shrivel, to dry. They twanged and snapped like vines drying in the summer heat.

As they watched, the physical form of the Nestene

Consciousness began to crack, spilling out a green froth. It erupted in a dozen, a hundred places, bursting, popping, finally dissolving on the floor, steaming and noxious. Green fumes filled the Atrium, smelling of molten plastic and the stench of alien flesh.

The whole process had taken a little under ten seconds.

Beneath the endless torrents of water, the Doctor and Sir Gerry slowly picked themselves up, the Doctor nodding in gratitude at Chantelle and Reece.

There was silence in the Plaza, apart from the endless rushing of the water.

Chantelle's phone warbled.

She answered it. 'Hello?'

The Doctor held his breath.

Chantelle looked up at the Doctor and smiled. 'It's Kate,' she said. 'She's fine.'

FIFTEEN

'**P**oof!' said Sir Gerry, throwing his hands up in the air in despair.

Kate Maguire looked away from the office picture window, where she was standing and watching a vast clean-up operation. 'Beg your pardon, Sir Gerry?'

'*Poof!*' he said again. 'All gone! One mad night, lass, and there goes years of work.' He sighed, folded his arms, came to stand beside her at the window. 'Good job this place was insured,' he muttered.

Kate laughed. 'What – against extraterrestrial attack?'

'I'm sure there's summat in't small print,' he growled, knocking back a double whisky, then pouring another for himself and one for Kate. 'You can't be too careful these days. Anyways, I'm not convinced. I think they were terrorists, meself.'

Kate shook her head in disbelief. 'You know, I'm starting to see what the Doctor means about us.'

'Damn good fettling, this place is going to get,' said Sir Gerry, nodding. 'Then it can be used again! Think of all the positives!'

Down below them, bustling activity had been going on for several hours under emergency lighting. Vacuum drains had removed most of the water, Kate saw, although some puddles lingered.

Camouflaged operatives in gas masks were carrying the Auton remains away in translucent, coffin-like pods. Forensic teams were all over the shattered shop windows, taking samples. Vast areas of Hyperville had been sealed off with opaque white plastic. Above the complex, helicopters clattered ominously.

Within an hour of the defeat of the Consciousness, a uniformed military squad had arrived, cutting through the Hyperville blast-doors and filling the malls and boulevards with lorries and jeeps. The officer in charge, her eyes covered by reflective sunglasses, had told Sir Gerry in no uncertain terms that he was to stay in his office and be prepared to give a full report. They would have removed Kate from the site, but Sir Gerry had insisted that she was his assistant and she had to stay.

Now, in his office, Sir Gerry offered Kate her glass of whisky. 'So – get a good story in the end, did you?' Sir Gerry asked her casually.

'What?' She was momentarily nonplussed.

Sir Gerry chortled. 'I didn't come down in't last shower, love. I know an undercover hack when I see one. Rumbled you right from the start. Thought I'd let you get on with it. See what you turned up.'

'Oh. Right.' Kate blushed, and took a sip of the strong, harsh whisky to cover her embarrassment.

'Nowt to be sorry about. You did a good job. I'd rather have you working for me any day over any of those pushy business-school types. "Giving it 110 per cent", indeed.' Sir Gerry snorted, then chuckled.

Kate grinned. 'Well, quite. Anyone who says they're giving 110 per cent can drop their effort by a tenth and still claim to be giving their all. They never think about that.'

'Quite so!'

'So,' Kate said, 'what now? For you? I mean – it's all over, isn't it?'

'Don't be daft, lass! I've got fingers in hundreds more pies. Literally, in fact. Mrs Bidney's Steak-and-Kidneys? Know them? Bestselling frozen pastry goods on the market?'

Kate nodded. She had seen the adverts. 'You've got a share in those?' she asked, impressed.

'Miss Maguire, I *am* Mrs Bidney's Steak-and-Kidneys. I had 51 per cent of the bloomin' shares. Bought the beggars out in a hostile takeover just before Christmas. We're about to crack the USA.' Sir Gerry chuckled. 'Never put all your eggs into one basket, lass. That's my first rule of business.'

Kate decided not to challenge him on the various 'first rules' of business she had heard over the past few days. She put her hands behind her back and swivelled on one heel. 'Sir Gerry? I've… been having a few thoughts.'

'Oh, yes?'

'This place… It was never right. Oh, I know people came here, spent money, but… well… all that artificial stuff. Plastic wonderlands and so on. Not very twenty-first century really. Not very eco.'

Sir Gerry narrowed his eyes. 'What did you have in mind?'

'I'm thinking mega-green,' said Kate, eyes shining excitedly. 'Wind-powered, solar-powered eco-complexes. All in the open air. Renewable energy sources, recycled materials…' She smiled. 'It would be great to have your backing for something like that.'

Sir Gerry clapped her hard on the shoulder, making her wince. 'By 'eck, Kate. This could be the beginning of a beautiful partnership. And what about that Doctor feller? Will he want in on it?'

Kate put her glass down and extricated herself from Sir Gerry. 'That reminds me. Two ticks.' She waved at him as she hurried to the door. The soldier on guard outside immediately stepped forward to bar her way, but she put her hands on her hips sternly. 'I need the *loo*,' she snarled. 'I get very, very tetchy if I don't get to go when I need it.'

The young soldier looked nervously up and down the corridor, then nodded reluctantly and let her past.

The Doctor was beckoning.

'Slowly… Slowly… Whoa! Stop!'

The four soldiers who had pushed the TARDIS out of one of Hyperville's few functioning lifts for him nodded, and stomped off, grumbling amongst themselves. The Doctor smiled in satisfaction, patting the battered blue paintwork of the police box.

'Am I interrupting something?' said a familiar voice.

The Doctor looked up the length of the wrecked mall. Kate Maguire was there, looking immaculate again, arms folded and smiling impishly.

'Oh! Kate. Hello!'

'Wondering where you'd got to.'

'Oh… well… I was just going to…' The Doctor gestured vaguely. 'You know. Slip off. This place is going to be taken apart by UNIT now. They tend to ask all sorts of dull questions, and want *reports* and things.' He bobbed his head as if weighing it up. 'Not really my scene,' he admitted.

'You won't get out,' said Kate, amused. 'That UNIT woman – what's she called, Magambo? – she's got all the entrances cordoned off. Nobody leaves without a debriefing, she said to Sir Gerry.'

'Rrrright. Well, I don't do that kind of thing… Oh! Reece and Chantelle! Are they OK?'

'Fine,' said Kate with a smile. 'They found their mum. She'd done a runner when the alarms went off. Didn't want to leave, but got swept up in the crowd. Was going spare that she couldn't find them.' Kate frowned. 'Doctor… What about Shaneeqi? Do you think…'

The Doctor came to stand over her and looked down as if he knew what she was going to say. 'Do I think what?'

'Do you think there are any more? Or were she and Kendrick the only ones?'

'Time will tell,' said the Doctor. 'Not a lot we can do about it. Anyway, with the Nestene Consciousness itself destroyed, there's no central neural pathway to its influence any more. So if there is anyone else… perhaps their autonomy is finally complete.'

'So they might never know.'

'No.'

'Imagine that, though. I mean, your life…you *know* it's real, don't you? You've lived it. How can it be faked? All those memories. Smells, tastes, things that bring back your childhood.' She looked up at him. 'Do you remember *your* childhood?'

The Doctor looked embarrassed, rubbed his nose. 'Some of it,' he said awkwardly. 'Ah! Now, then. Something to do.' He fished in his pocket and waggled the Hypercard at her. 'I've got to get this back to your 16-year-old self, so that you can give it to me a few hours ago. If you see what I mean!' He opened the police box door and popped inside. 'Won't be a minute,' he said.

Kate wrinkled her nose. 'But isn't that a—'

The door slammed shut.

A second later there was a great rushing wind, ruffling Kate's clothes and making her take a step backwards. The debris all around rustled and skittered – and with a terrible noise, like the shearing of metal mixed in with the trumpeting of a hundred elephants, the blue box became transparent and faded from view.

Kate blinked.

She rubbed her eyes.

She shrugged, and turned to walk away.

Then, at the edge of her hearing, there was the noise again, as if reaching back through immeasurable distances.

Kate looked back over her shoulder. The rubbish and the fragments of plaster and tattered clothes were whipped up into a whirlpool again. And there, in the mall, just a few metres from where it had disappeared, the police box returned in a bright whirlpool of blue light.

The lamp on the top stopped flashing and the door opened. The Doctor sauntered out, hands in pockets, looking satisfied.

'—time paradox, yes, very probably,' he said, finishing

Kate's sentence for her. He shrugged. 'I wouldn't worry. They all sort themselves out in the end.'

'Right,' she said. 'Um… gosh. OK.'

'You're lost for words. I like that. You're not often lost for words. Good to have new experiences, I always think. Well, apart from chilli-and-chocolate crisps. I mean, what were *they* all about?'

She didn't answer.

'No. OK. Well.' The Doctor cleared his throat awkwardly. 'Anyway, look, I appreciated all your help.'

Kate shrugged, smiled. 'That's OK. I'm… looking forward to working with you again.'

'Aaah, well…' He nodded towards the open door of his police box. 'I'd normally, um, offer to give you a little trip somewhere. As a kind of thank you. But at the moment, I'm… sort of experimenting with… travelling alone.' He scratched his ear awkwardly, swivelled on one heel and looked at a point just beyond her head. 'Seeing how it works out.' He swallowed uncomfortably. 'You know. Easy come, easy go, and all that.'

Kate nodded. 'Oh, yes, OK. My friend Oliver's doing that. He's backpacking through Eastern Europe.'

'Rrrrright. I tend to go a bit further afield than that. Although the Berlin Wall coming down was fun. I did that twice.'

'*Twice*?'

'Yeah, I… um…' He scratched his ear and looked abashed. 'I went back again. So I could be sure I missed David Hasselhoff singing. Anyway. Look. Maybe we'll see each other again.'

Kate shrugged. 'Maybe,' she said with a smile.

'You'll be busy. No doubt. Got plenty of ideas up your sleeve.'

She smiled. 'Plenty.'

'Right, well, I'll be off, then.' He stood in the doorway and waved. 'Going. Disappearing.'

And this time, he really did.

The blue door shut behind him and the sound began again. Like some engine from beyond reality, it shuddered and juddered. Its unearthly, trumpeting howl echoed up into the scarred atrium of Hyperville, long after the box itself had vanished.

Kate took her hands away from her ears. Then she sat and waited, perched on a bench, eating an apple.

She waited for an hour, but he didn't come back.

Eventually, a soldier, one of the clean-up team, put a hand on her arm and asked politely if she wouldn't mind moving. As if breaking out of a deep reverie, she nodded.

Kate Maguire straightened herself up, buttoned her jacket and turned and walked away.

Into the future.

On Hyperion Boulevard, they were finishing clearing up.

Soldiers rushed to and fro, their gloved hands picking up debris and putting it into sealed containers for analysis. The malls rang with shouted instructions, with the clattering of booted feet.

An Auton lay abandoned, its fashionable clothing in rags, its head misshapen. Its arms were splayed out, with the semi-solid plastic stuck to the floor like stringy cheese fondue.

Slowly, weakly, as if using its last residue of power, the Auton's twisted hands began to clench and unclench. Its head lifted up from the floor, stretchy flesh unsticking from the marble floor with a plasticky ripping sound. And then, as if the effort was too much, its head flopped back down on to the floor, and its body went limp.

But its eyes still glowed with the dimmest of pink light, like a dying sunset.

Acknowledgements

For all the children who have ever watched *Doctor Who* with me – especially Elinor, Samuel, Laura, Xander, Miranda and Emma.

Thanks to the people who helped to get me into gear and get this book written: Justin Richards, Gary Russell, all at BBC Books, and my agent Caroline Montgomery. Also to Martin Day for sensible words when they were needed, and David Llewellyn for biting humour. As always, many thanks to Rachel for her love and patience.

A respectful nod to the late Robert Holmes, the Auton-Meister – I hope I have done them justice.

And of course, this book could not exist without the imagination and resourcefulness of Russell T Davies, David Tennant and the team who, over the last five years, have brought *Doctor Who* to a whole new generation. *Allons-y.*

DOCTOR · WHO

Also available from BBC Books
featuring the Doctor
as played by David Tennant:

DOCTOR·WHO

The Eyeless
by Lance Parkin
ISBN 978 1 846 07562 9
£6.99

At the heart of the ruined city of Arcopolis is the Fortress. It's a brutal structure placed here by one of the sides in a devastating intergalactic war that's long ended. Fifteen years ago, the entire population of the planet was killed in an instant by the weapon housed deep in the heart of the Fortress. Now only the ghosts remain.

The Doctor arrives, and determines to fight his way past the Fortress's automatic defences and put the weapon beyond use. But he soon discovers he's not the only person in Arcopolis. What is the true nature of the weapon? Is the planet really haunted? Who are the Eyeless? And what will happen if they get to the weapon before the Doctor?

The Doctor has a fight on his hands. And this time he's all on his own.

Elvis the King Spaceport has grown into the sprawling
city-state of New Memphis – an urban jungle, where
organised crime is rife. But the launch of the new
Terminal 13 hasn't been as smooth as expected. And
things are about to get worse...

When the Doctor arrives, he finds the whole terminal
locked down. The notorious Invisible Assassin is at work
again, and the Judoon troopers sent to catch him will stop
at nothing to complete their mission.

With the assassin loose on the mean streets of New
Memphis, the Doctor is forced into a strange alliance.
Together with teenage private eye Nikki and a ruthless
Judoon Commander, the Doctor soon discovers that
things are even more complicated – and dangerous – than
he first thought...

Also available from BBC Books
featuring the Doctor
as played by David Tennant:

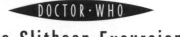

DOCTOR·WHO

The Slitheen Excursion
by Simon Guerrier
ISBN 978 1 846 07640 4
£6.99

1500BC – King Actaeus and his subjects live in mortal fear of the awesome gods who have come to visit their kingdom in ancient Greece. Except the Doctor, visiting with university student June, knows they're not gods at all. They're aliens.

For the aliens, it's the perfect holiday – they get to tour the sights of a primitive planet and even take part in local customs. Like gladiatorial games, or hunting down and killing humans who won't be missed.

With June's enthusiastic help, the Doctor soon meets the travel agents behind this deadly package holiday company – his old enemies the Slitheen. But can he bring the Slitheen excursion to an end without endangering more lives? And how are events in ancient Greece linked to a modern-day alien plot to destroy what's left of the Parthenon?

DOCTOR·WHO

Prisoner of the Daleks

by Trevor Baxendale
ISBN 978 1 846 07641 1
£6.99

The Daleks are advancing, their empire constantly
expanding into Earth's space. The Earth forces are resisting
the Daleks in every way they can. But the battles rage on
across countless solar systems. And now the future of our
galaxy hangs in the balance…

The Doctor finds himself stranded on board a starship
near the frontline with a group of ruthless bounty hunters.
Earth Command will pay them for every Dalek they kill,
every eye stalk they bring back as proof.

With the Doctor's help, the bounty hunters achieve the
ultimate prize: a Dalek prisoner – intact, powerless, and
ready for interrogation. But where the Daleks are involved,
nothing is what it seems, and no one is safe. Before long
the tables will be turned, and how will the Doctor survive
when he becomes a prisoner of
the Daleks?

DOCTOR · WHO

The Taking of Chelsea 426

by David Llewellyn
ISBN 978 1 846 07758 6
£6.99

The Chelsea Flower Show – hardly the most exciting or
dangerous event in the calendar, or so the Doctor thinks.
But this is Chelsea 426, a city-sized future colony floating
on the clouds of Saturn, and the flowers are much more
than they seem.

As the Doctor investigates, he becomes more and more
worried. Why is shopkeeper Mr Pemberton acting so
strangely? And what is Professor Wilberforce's terrible
secret?

They are close to finding the answers when a familiar foe
arrives, and the stakes suddenly get much higher. The
Sontarans have plans of their own, and they're not here to
arrange flowers…

DOCTOR·WHO

The Krillitane Storm
by Christopher Cooper
ISBN 978 1 846 07761 6
£6.99

When the TARDIS materialises in medieval Worcester,
the Doctor finds the city seemingly deserted. He soon
discovers its population are living in a state of terror,
afraid to leave their homes after dark, for fear of meeting
their doom at the hands of the legendary Devil's
Huntsman.

For months, people have been disappearing, and the
Sheriff has imposed a strict curfew across the city,
his militia maintaining control over the superstitious
populace with a firm hand, closing the city to outsiders.
Is it fear of attack from beyond the city walls that drives
him or the threat closer to home? Or does the Sheriff have
something to hide?

After a terrifying encounter with a deadly Krillitane, the
Doctor realises the city has good reason to be scared.

Also available from BBC Books:

DOCTOR·WHO

MONSTERS AND VILLAINS
by Justin Richards

ALIENS AND ENEMIES
by Justin Richards

CREATURES AND DEMONS
by Justin Richards

STARSHIPS AND SPACESTATIONS
by Justin Richards

THE SHOOTING SCRIPTS
by Russell T Davies,
Mark Gatiss, Robert Shearman,
Paul Cornell and Steven Moffat

THE INSIDE STORY
by Gary Russell

THE ENCYCLOPEDIA
by Gary Russell

THE TIME TRAVELLER'S ALMANAC
by Steve Tribe

Also available from BBC Books:

DOCTOR·WHO

Companions and Allies
by Steve Tribe
ISBN 978 1 846 07749 4
£7.99

The Doctor has been travelling through space and time for centuries, showing his friends and companions the wonders of the universe. From Sarah Jane Smith and the Brigadier to Martha Jones and Donna Noble, *Companions and Allies* celebrates the friends who have been by his side and the heroes that have helped him battle his deadliest foes. Find out:

- How the First Doctor uprooted schoolteachers Ian and Barbara from their twentieth-century lives
- Why the Third Doctor worked for UNIT
- How the Fifth Doctor sacrificed his life for Peri
- Who helped the Eighth Doctor save Earth from the Master
- What became of Rose Tyler and her family

And much more. Beautifully illustrated and including – for the first time – a complete story guide to the adventures of all ten Doctors, this is the definitive guide to the Doctor's intergalactic family.

DOCTOR·WHO

The Ultimate Monster Guide
by Justin Richards
ISBN 978 1 846 07745 6
£14.99

With *The Ultimate Monster Guide*, *Doctor Who* historian Justin Richards has created the most comprehensive guide to the Doctor's enemies ever published. With fully illustrated entries that cover everything from Adipose and Autons to Zarbi and Zygons, this guide tells you everything you need to know about the many dastardly creatures the Doctor has fought since he first appeared on television.

Featuring a wealth of material from the current and classic series, the guide also includes behind-the-scenes secrets of how the monsters were created, as well as design drawings and images. Find out how the Cybermen were redesigned over the years, and how Davros was resurrected to lead his Daleks once again. Discover the computer magic that made the Beast possible, and the make-up wizardry that created the Weeping Angels. Learn how many incarnations of the Master the Doctor has encountered, and which other misguided Time Lords he has defeated…

Lavishly designed with photos and artwork throughout, *The Ultimate Monster Guide* is essential reading for all travellers in time and space!